Kate McManus

EVEN IN HEAVEN...

Melody can't sleep. Every time she closes her eyes, she sees the vision of herself and Chaz back on Earth, on their mission to Scarlett's school. It's Chaz's first day there, and Scarlett has zeroed in on him like a hawk on its prey.

She has that same gleam in her eye tonight, Melody thought. *Scarlett is scared and mad, still having a hard time believing that she's dead.*

But mad, and scared, and dead, Scarlett is looking at Chaz the same way she looked at him down below. She wants him.

And Melody knows there isn't a thing she can do about it.

Other Avon Flare Books in the
TEEN ANGELS *Series by*
Cherie Bennett and Jeff Gottesfeld

ANGEL KISSES
HEAVEN CAN'T WAIT
LOVE NEVER DIES
HEAVEN HELP US!

Coming Soon

LOVE WITHOUT END

Avon Books are available at special quantity discounts for bulk purchases for sales promotions, premiums, fund raising or educational use. Special books, or book excerpts, can also be created to fit specific needs.

For details write or telephone the office of the Director of Special Markets, Avon Books, Dept. FP, 1350 Avenue of the Americas, New York, New York 10019, 1-800-238-0658.

TEEN ANGELS

#5

NIGHTMARE IN HEAVEN

CHERIE BENNETT
and JEFF GOTTESFELD

AN AVON FLARE BOOK

If you purchased this book without a cover, you should be aware that this book is stolen property. It was reported as "unsold and destroyed" to the publisher, and neither the author nor the publisher has received any payment for this "stripped book."

TEEN ANGELS #5: NIGHTMARE IN HEAVEN is an original publication of Avon Books. This work has never before appeared in book form. While certain characters and events in the story are real, they are used here fictitiously.

AVON BOOKS
A division of
The Hearst Corporation
1350 Avenue of the Americas
New York, New York 10019

Copyright © 1996 by Cherie Bennett and Jeff Gottesfeld
Published by arrangement with the authors
Library of Congress Catalog Card Number: 95-96211
ISBN: 0-380-78578-1
RL: 6.7

All rights reserved, which includes the right to reproduce this book or portions thereof in any form whatsoever except as provided by the U.S. Copyright Law. For information address Charlotte Sheedy Literary Agency, Inc., 41 King Street, New York, New York 10014.

First Avon Flare Printing: July 1996

AVON FLARE TRADEMARK REG. U.S. PAT. OFF. AND IN OTHER COUNTRIES, MARCA REGISTRADA, HECHO EN U.S.A.

Printed in the U.S.A.

RA 10 9 8 7 6 5 4 3 2 1

For Regula, with gratitude

NIGHTMARE IN HEAVEN

One

"The way I see it, ya'll, death has some real advantages over life," Cisco McCaine drawled, sitting up on the beach blanket in order to spread more suntan lotion on her arms and legs. Her two best friends, Nicole Van Owen and Melody Monroe, stared at her as if she had just grown two heads.

"Cisco!" Nicole said in a horrified tone of voice, her long red hair shimmering as she bolted up to face Cisco. "How can you possibly say that?"

A couple of gorgeous guys walked past their blanket.

"*That*, for example," Cisco said, her eyes following the guys down the beach.

"That simply isn't logical," Nicole insisted. "There are plenty of guys on Earth."

"Not as fine as those two," Cisco decided, still watching the two guys as they began to throw a Frisbee back and forth.

Melody, who looked so much like a young Marilyn Monroe that it was spooky, shook her head seriously. "I'd give anything to go back to Earth and be alive again," she said in her breathy voice.

"You do get to go back," Nicole pointed out to Melody. "On missions."

Melody shook her head. "I don't mean as a Teen Angel, I mean as a human being."

"Oh, chill out, ya'll," Cisco said with a laugh, raising her voice to compete with the sound of a flock of seagulls flying overhead. "I was only kidding."

"Oh," Nicole said, lying back down on the beach blanket and repositioning her sunglasses. "I thought you were serious."

"That's only because you take everything too seriously," Cisco said, closing her eyes to enjoy the hot rays of the sun on her face. "Hey, do you think we're closer to the sun now that we're in Teen Heaven? I wonder how that works..."

Melody looked down at her thighs and frowned. "Do I look fat in this bathing suit?" she asked her friends anxiously.

Nicole groaned. "Melody, you are gorgeous. How could you possibly look fat?"

"I ate so much for lunch..." Melody mused anxiously.

"Yes, you're a huge whale," Cisco deadpanned. "When you hit the beach, I'm surprised everyone didn't start yelling 'Free Willy! Free Willy!'"

Melody blushed. "I know I get neurotic about it," she admitted.

Nicole touched her hand lightly. "Mel, you look fine. Honest."

"Thanks," Melody said gratefully.

"You know, when I *was* alive," Cisco began, "we had to drive all day and half the night to go to the beach in Florida."

"And here in Teen Heaven all JD has to do is snap his fingers, and we're here!" Melody pointed out.

"I still don't get how he did that," Nicole commented.

"There's a lot I don't get about this place," Cisco surmised, stretching out in the warm sunshine. "But, I say, hey, it's a day at Teen Heaven beach. Enjoy it."

"Pass me the sunscreen," Nicole said to Cisco, who took the tube of Coppertone and tossed it to her friend. "I don't want to get cancer."

"You're dead," Cisco reminded her, "you can't get cancer."

"How do you know?" Nicole pointed out, spreading the sun-warmed lotion up and down her long, pale legs.

"I don't think JD ever told us about getting cancer," Melody said slowly, "but there are kids who miss school at Teen Heaven High with colds. And they're dead, too."

"Sheesh," Cisco said. "Ya'll, you only live once. And you did already. Just enjoy the day."

Melody stretched out on the blanket, listened to the waves of the ocean roll in, and thought for the millionth time about the astonishing circumstances that had landed her in Teen Heaven.

If only people really knew what happens to you when you die, like Cisco and Nicole and I know, Melody reflected. *The world would be a totally different place.*

Of course, sometimes Teen Heaven is so much like

Earth that it's scary, Melody thought. *Like today. Who would have thought there'd be a beach here? Of course, if you think about it, why shouldn't there be a beach here?*

Melody sighed quietly, and thought back to her former life, when she was an eighteen-year-old teenager—and alive—in Detroit, Michigan. She couldn't help it that as she grew up, she looked and sounded more and more like Marilyn Monroe every day.

And she couldn't help it that her parents had divorced when she was ten years old, and that her mother, who'd never learned any real skills, had to struggle to make ends meet as a waitress after her dad took off.

She couldn't even help it when her mother began to look to her, and especially to her incredible looks, as the salvation for the family. Her mother started taking her out for print modeling jobs when Melody was twelve years old, and by the time Melody was fourteen, she was earning five times as much as a model than her mother ever did as a waitress in the diner.

Which is why her mother had quit her waitress job, to manage Melody's "career." Melody couldn't really help that, either.

But I hated modeling, Melody thought. *And I never really stuck up for myself. And I hated that my mother was constantly stopping me from eating, so that I wouldn't get fat. She was so sure that I was going to become this really famous movie star and make her rich, when I didn't really care about being an actress at all!*

But as Melody gazed out at the ocean breakers, rolling in, one after another, she remembered yet again that there was one thing that she could help: she didn't have to get into the car with her then-boyfriend Buddy, who had insisted that he drive her home after a date, when Melody knew that he was already really drunk.

Buddy drove. The car crashed.

Buddy lived, Melody died.

End of story.

Almost.

Because Melody woke up in Teen Heaven.

She hadn't been in Teen Heaven very long now, but it had been long enough to learn a few things.

First, Teen Heaven was a lot like Earth. There was a high school for her to go to, there was the Mall Over America for shopping, there was her new after-school job at the Rock Around the Cloud Cafe, there was even a Teen Angel guy, Chaz Denton, whom Melody loved.

Second, Teen Heaven wasn't very much like Earth at all. It was run by a guy named JD, who looked as much like the old movie star James Dean as Melody looked like Marilyn Monroe, and JD had a direct line straight to the Big Guy.

And everyone knew who the Big Guy was.

JD ran the Teen Heaven show for the Big Guy. He was the one who gave the girls their missions, back Down Below. And he was the one who could snap his fingers and send the entire student body of Teen Heaven High School for a day at the beach. Just like he had done today.

JD was the one, presumably, who had decided that Melody, Nicole, and Cisco would be roommates in a single suite in one of the girls' dorms.

Now, that was one great decision, Melody thought happily, looking at her two friends, who'd both closed their eyes, their faces up to the sun.

The three of us are so different, Melody mused. *Cisco comes from a tiny town in Tennessee. She's smart, and tough, and a rebel, and she dresses like it. When she came out of alcohol rehab, she found out her boyfriend had cheated on her. So she got mad, and drove her motorcycle without wearing a helmet.*

Now, she's here.

And Nicole, she's nearly perfect. Perfect red hair, perfect long legs . . . her parents are professors at the University of Pennsylvania, she's from a Main Line family in Philadelphia, and everyone thought she was going to go to Penn, too, Melody recalled, looking down at her friend, who was idly running sand through her fingers.

Then, she messed up her SATs. And took an overdose of sleeping pills so she wouldn't have to face her parents.

Now, she's here. In Teen Heaven with me.

JD had explained to them all how Teen Heaven worked: teens were sent to Teen Heaven if they died Down Below with life lessons left to learn. They had to learn some of these lessons in Teen Heaven and some of them Down Below, on their missions.

Yes, missions.

The Big Guy sent each Teen Angel down to Earth periodically on an assignment, where the Teen Angel would try to affect the life of a teen in trouble so the teen would make positive choices. If the mission succeeded, the Teen Angel got points on his or her Angel Card.

Enough points, JD had said, and you're into Ultimate Heaven, which he always said was "so cool you couldn't even envision such coolness."

But, Melody thought, *people on Earth have it all wrong about angels.*

We don't have magical powers when we go down on missions.

We can't appear and disappear.

And we certainly don't have wings.

All we have is knowledge. JD says that knowl—

"Hi kids!" a loud chirpy voice called from behind Melody. Melody sighed, since she knew that voice could only belong to one person—the biggest suck-up in Teen Heaven, the one, the only, Celeste Durkey.

Celeste's blonde curls bounced as she plopped herself down, uninvited, on the girls' blanket. "So, how's every little thing?" Celeste asked, reaching for their suntan lotion and squirting it liberally on her legs.

"We *were* enjoying the day," Cisco said pointedly.

Celeste took off the t-shirt she was wearing, and Melody heard Cisco stifle a snort when she saw the swimsuit Celeste had chosen. It was hot pink and covered with huge, white smiley faces.

"Gee, nice suit," Cisco said, trying to keep a straight face.

"Oh, jeepers, thanks!" Celeste said. "I have twenty bathing suits, did you know that? One is light blue with orange ruffles, one is yellow with little ducklings on the neckline—"

"We get the idea," Nicole said politely.

"Guess what!" Celeste said happily, her doll-like blue eyes shining under her mop of curly blonde hair.

"What?" Melody asked.

"You know that I was assigned a single room before?" Celeste said. "In the dorm?"

"Yup," Cisco responded. "I know."

"Next door to us," Nicole pointed out.

"How could we possibly forget?" Cisco added. Melody nudged her in the ribs, as if to say "don't-be-so-mean."

"Well, here's the news, are you ready?" Celeste asked with excitement. "I'm getting a new roommate! JD told me himself!"

As if on cue, JD materialized on the beach right in front of the girls. He had on baggy sky-blue surfer jams and wraparound sunglasses.

"Ladies," he said, tipping his head to them, "how goes it this fine day at the beach?"

"Super!" Celeste chirped.

His gaze fell on her.

"Where did you find *that*?" he asked curiously, eyeing her bathing suit.

"Mall Over America!" Celeste answered proudly. "Yesterday."

JD took his little notebook out of his back pocket and jotted something down in it. "Remind me to speak to the manager of Sun 'N Sand," he said.

"You know, I've never seen you in anything except jeans before," Melody noted, eyeing JD.

"Hey, a little sun never hurt anyone," JD said.

"It doesn't matter what you wear," Cisco said, stretching out her legs. "You still look just like James Dean."

Melody nodded in agreement.

Just like James Dean in that movie Cisco rented for us, she recalled, *Rebel Without a Cause*.

"When are you going to 'fess up and just admit you *are* him?" Cisco asked, her head cocked to the side.

"Yeah!" Celeste agreed. She patted the blanket next to her. "You can sit right here and tell us everything."

"Please, ladies," JD chided them. "All play and no work makes JD a bad supervisor. And I don't want to get assigned to go run Deep Six."

All four girls shuddered. Deep Six was the alternative to Teen Heaven. The *bad* alternative. It was supposed to be horrible. Cisco had even met a girl from Deep Six on one of her missions, and she was more horrible and scary than creatures from the scariest horror novels she'd ever read.

"Hey, JD, JD," Celeste called, wriggling around with excitement. "I'm getting a roommate, right JD?"

"Affirmative," JD acknowledged, "and—"

"—and I'm moving!" Celeste yelled gleefully, sort of as if she'd just won the Lotto back on Earth.

Melody saw Nicole and Cisco trade guarded looks. Celeste had recently been transferred into the single directly next door to the girls' suite. And, ever since she'd arrived, they'd been subject to a Celeste Durkey barrage of unannounced visits, sappy little post-it notes on their doors, and the sickening, wafting smell of the strawberry incense that Celeste burned in her room from time to time.

If Celeste was moving, maybe there was a chance that she was moving out of their—

"Right into that room across the hall from you guys!" Celeste continued. "Isn't that super?"

Oh well, Melody thought, as she saw Cisco and

Nicole's dejected faces. *I can put up with her if I have to. At least there'll be someone living with her to distract her away from us.*

"I know how happy you all are about that," Celeste continued, totally clueless as to their real feelings about her. "And that means I can continue to inspect your room for mess and sloth. I keep a checklist in my room so I always know my room is as perfectly groomed as I am. I keep copies of the list in my—"

"Stifle it, Celeste," JD interrupted. "We catch the drift."

"So, who's the new arrival, JD?" Cisco asked casually.

"JD told me all about her!" Celeste said, cutting off JD before he could get a word out. "She died about an hour ago, in a house fire Down Below. So she's making The Journey now."

JD nodded his head affirmatively. "Lavender is meeting her in the Transit Room," he said.

"She's from your state," Celeste said to Cisco, "from Tennessee. And she has a dog."

"That's nice," Melody said with a smile. "I just hope it gets along with Ruffy."

One of the best parts of Teen Heaven, Melody had always thought, is that Teen Angels got reunited there with pets who had died before they did. Or, if they didn't have a pet, they were given either a dog or a cat by JD soon after they arrived. That was how Melody had acquired her little cat, Ruffy.

"The dog has the strangest name," Celeste said, reaching for Cisco's sunscreen again.

"What is it?" Nicole asked.

"Pickles," Celeste said. "Can you imagine naming your dog *Pickles*?"

Melody's jaw dropped involuntarily.

The dog's name is Pickles? she thought. *But that was the name of Scarlett Whitmore's dog. Scarlett was the subject of my first mission down below, and she was only the nastiest, most hateful, meanest, coldest—*

By the time she got to the end of the thought, Melody was as white as a sheet. She looked up at JD, fearful of what he might say.

All he did was shake his head sympathetically.

"No, no, it can't be—" Melody began.

"I don't get to pick who comes here or goes to Deep Six," JD said with a shrug. "And Scarlett Whitmore's coming to Teen Heaven."

"But . . . but she's terrible!" Melody exclaimed. "She's hateful!"

"Hey, ours is not to question the decisions of the Big Guy," JD reminded Melody gently. "Am I right or am I right?"

"I know," Melody said with a sigh. "It's just that . . ." Her voice trailed off. There really wasn't anything to say.

"Great rays," JD said, lifting his head to the sun. Then he turned to Melody. "So, I suggest you get yourself ready. You and Chaz, that is."

"Why?" Melody asked guardedly. Back down on Earth, Scarlett had flirted outrageously with Melody's boyfriend, Chaz, which had made Melody absolutely crazy with insecurity and jealousy.

"Seeing as you and Chaz know Scarlett, you guys will be the head of Scarlett's welcoming committee," JD said breezily.

"But—" Melody began to protest.

"Uh, uh, uh!" JD admonished, shaking his head. "Ours in not to question why, babe. You know what I always say—"

"Live, die, and learn," the four girls intoned together. Cisco rolled her eyes.

JD grinned. "So glad to see my message is getting through. So, gotta fly—in my case I mean that literally," JD said, laughing at his own joke. "Good luck with Scarlett, Melody." He snapped his fingers and disappeared.

Cisco, Nicole, and Celeste all stared at Melody.

"It's bad, huh?" Cisco asked.

"Worse than that," Melody said.

"Well, I don't care what you say!" Celeste cried, jumping up. "Scarlett is my new roommate and I'm sure she's wonderful!"

Melody closed her eyes wearily. Celeste Durkey and Scarlett Whitmore were both going to be living right across the hall from her.

Death couldn't get much worse.

Two

"Free, do I really have to do this?" Melody asked, sitting down at the table where her dorm's housemother, Freida (who liked to be called Free), was already sitting. Melody's boyfriend, Chaz Denton, sat at the table, too, sipping a Coke.

"Yep, you gotta," Free nodded, taking a sip of the herbal tea that Melody had served her not ten minutes before. "So I suggest you hang loose." Free was a hippie who had died in a hot-air balloon accident over the original Woodstock, and she clung to her old hippie vernacular.

"Hang loose?" Chaz repeated. "This girl hated Mel's guts Down Below!"

"Yeah, she'll hate them now, too," Free affirmed. "But JD told me that you two are supposed to greet her here, so don't even think about splitting!"

It was later that day, around six-thirty in the evening, after JD had brought everyone back to town—with a snap of his fingers—after their day at the beach. Everyone in Teen Heaven had part-time jobs, and Melody had recently started hers at Rock Around the Cloud Cafe.

Rock Around the Cloud was right on Teen Heaven's main drag, the recently-renamed Salk Street, about a mile down from Teen Heaven High School. Free had called her at work to tell her she needed to plan about an hour break from her duties.

The cafe was modeled on a late-1950s diner, and, for all Melody knew, it had been around that long. There were many round and square tables in the center, and red leatherette booths around the sides. There was a row of red stools in front of a long formica counter, behind which four teens were currently making ice cream sodas and flipping hamburgers for the big early evening crowd.

And along one wall, there was a long row of old-fashioned pinball machines, and a jukebox dominated by music from the 1950s and 1960s.

Melody loved working here. It was a very popular spot with the teens of Teen Heaven, JD himself dropped in frequently, and, best of all, the place was run entirely by teenagers.

There was no "boss." Everyone just seemed to know their job, and do it well. And they did it wearing '50s-style clothing of their own choice. For example, today Melody's outfit was a baby pink sweater set with little pearl buttons, and a circular pink felt skirt with a poodle embroidered on it. On her feet she wore pink and white saddle shoes.

People might say I'm crazy, Melody thought with a little smile, *but I like working at Rock*

Around the Cloud much better than I liked modeling back on Earth.

Free looked down at her watch, which Melody had a hard time seeing because of the thirty or so bangle bracelets that dangled from Free's forearm.

"Scarlett's due here in ten minutes," Free announced. "Sunny himself's bringing her over. She had a rough Journey, I understand."

"Ten minutes," Melody sighed, reaching over to massage one of her calf muscles.

"Well," Chaz said to Free, "if we have to greet her, at least you and Sunny will be here."

Melody nodded grateful agreement. Sunny was Free's husband. Barrel-chested, deep-voiced, and sporting an Afro hairdo so big he sometimes had difficulty entering a room, Sunny was smart, kind, and as fair-minded as the TAs could wish a house parent would be.

"Negative," Free said lightly. "You're on your own. Me and Sunny, we'll be outta here. How'd you meet this chick, anyway?"

"We told you already," Chaz said, slightly annoyed. "I just can't believe—"

"Hey, my memory's not so great, I did too many drugs in the sixties," Free replied.

"Did you, really?" Melody asked, wide-eyed.

"It was a joke," Free assured her. "My drug of choice was always sunshine and freedom, right on!"

"Right on," Chaz repeated tonelessly.

"So, talk the talk, my man," Free said, sipping her tea.

Together, Chaz and Melody recounted the

story of Melody's first mission back Down Below. JD had sent Melody down to Whitmore High School in Nashville, Tennessee, where Melody was to try to improve the attitude of Scarlett Whitmore, a gorgeous, rich, unhappy, and totally obnoxious girl who was used to getting her own way with everyone, including guys.

Melody had a hard time, so JD had sent Chaz to join Melody to give her some help. And Scarlett Whitmore had wasted no time in proceeding to make the very handsome Chaz Denton her new boyfriend, which drove Melody completely crazy.

I had a lot more luck with a girl who wasn't my mission than I did with Scarlett, Melody recalled. *Although I can't blame Scarlett for going after Chaz. He is so handsome. And sweet. And really, really nice. And such a talented artist!*

She looked over at Chaz Denton, who was the first guy she'd ever met—dead or alive—who seemed to appreciate Melody for more than her extraordinary appearance.

He looked back at her, his dark hair tumbling into his huge brown eyes, and smiled.

He even looks like a painter, Melody thought, *and*—

"Ready or not," Free interrupted Melody's thought, "here she comes." Free pointed to the glass entrance to Rock Around the Cloud, where Sunny had just led an unhappy-looking Scarlett Whitmore inside.

"Yo, Sunny!" a guy called out to him from behind the counter.

"Peace, bro," Sunny replied, flashing him the peace sign with his right hand.

"Hey Sunny, when do I get to take a razor to your head?" one of the waitresses asked.

Sunny grinned. "This 'fro?" he asked. "Nobody touches this 'fro but Free and me."

"Scarlett looks just the same," Chaz muttered under his breath, as Sunny led Scarlett to their table.

He took Melody's hand in his own and gave it a loving squeeze. Melody didn't let go.

"I'd forgotten how pretty she is," Melody whispered.

She looks exactly the same as when I first saw her, Melody thought. *Long, straight, honey-blonde hair, high cheekbones, thin nose, full lips. Expensive-looking clothes. And a snotty look on her face. That's Scarlett Whitmore.*

"I wonder how she got here." Chaz replied.

"Fire," Melody whispered.

And then Scarlett and Sunny were standing next to their table, looking down at them.

"Hi," Chaz said, standing up politely.

"Hello," Melody added, standing up next to Chaz.

Scarlett Whitmore just glared at them.

"Well, well, well, would you look at the time," Sunny said, ostentatiously looking at his watch. "I'm due back at the dorm to tutor Jake on his calc."

"But—" Melody began.

"We're outta here," Free said, getting up from the table and taking Sunny by the arm. "Peace and love!"

The two of them turned and left, leaving Chaz, Melody, and Scarlett standing by their table.

"Maybe we should sit down," Chaz said to

Melody, who nodded at him. The two of them sat down. Then, finally, Scarlett shrugged her shoulders, and sat down, too.

"Welcome to Teen Heaven," Melody said, gently. "Would you like a Coke or something?"

"This is some kinda joke, right?" Scarlett asked, tossing her hair. "Someone put LSD in the Jell-O at school or something?"

"No joke," Chaz said, taking a slug of his own Coke. "It's for real."

"That JD guy said I was dead, and that Lavender lady who met me when I woke up said I was dead," Scarlett said haughtily. "But I'm not dead, obviously, so I must be tripping."

Chaz and Melody looked at each other and shrugged simultaneously.

"And it's a really, really bad trip," Scarlett continued. "Because I never wanted to see either of you two ever again in my life."

Your wish came true, Melody wanted to say. But she bit her lip to keep her mouth shut.

There was a painfully long pause in the conversation, as Scarlett kept glancing around Rock Around the Cloud, and hitting herself in the head, as if one of the blows would knock her back to reality.

None did.

"You can stop hitting yourself," Melody said. "It won't change anything."

"How'd you get here?" Chaz asked, finally.

"How should I know?" Scarlett said, nastily. "The last thing I remember is getting into bed. Then Pickles jumped on the bed with me, because he always sleeps with me."

"You don't remember anything else?" Melody asked softly.

"That JD guy says my mother fell asleep with a burning cigarette in her hand," Scarlett said. Something flickered in her eyes, and for a moment she looked almost scared, almost, well, human. But the look left as quickly as it has come.

"He *says* the house burned down," Scarlett continued. "I'm *so* sure."

Melody took a couple of pieces of popcorn from the wicker basket on their table. "Ask JD to use the EarthScope," she suggested.

"The *what*?" Scarlett asked.

"EarthScope," Chaz said. "You give JD your Angel Card, he takes some points off it, and you get to look in on how things are going Down Below."

"Yeah, right," Scarlett scoffed, loudly, standing up at the table. "Look, isn't there something they can give me at the hospital to bring me down from this trip? Because I have had just about enough of this—"

"It's not a trip," Chaz said. "It's reality."

"You're only saying that because you're part of my trip," Scarlett informed him. "Which means I should not listen to anything that you say." She folded her arms.

"Look, I don't know how to convince you that this is real," Melody said earnestly, "but it is. "You're not on Earth anymore. You're dead. We're all dead."

Scarlett looked around the restaurant. All the employees and all the customers were watching her to see what she would do.

She studied them for a moment. Then she laughed. "This is some kind of major joke, right? Hey, I bet if that JD dude with the stupid hairdo snaps his fingers, he can show up here right now, standing on top of this table. Yeah, right."

Snap. Snap.

JD appeared on the table, his arms folded across his chest, a look on his face somewhere in between a grin and a smirk.

Snap. Snap.

JD disappeared.

The entire Rock Around the Cloud Cafe crowd burst into thunderous applause.

Scarlett Whitmore hit herself in the forehead again.

"Did you just see what I just saw?" she asked dizzily, falling back into her chair.

"And Scarlett, babe, a little piece of advice. Don't insult my 'do," JD's voice came, even though his body was nowhere in sight.

Scarlett's eyes grew huge. "Did you hear that?"

Melody and Chaz both nodded.

"I need a drink," Scarlett decided. "They serve beer here?"

"Drinking age is twenty-one in Teen Heaven," Melody recited, as she'd been instructed her first day on the job. "No exceptions."

"Please," Scarlett snorted sarcastically. She got up from the table and strode over to the counter.

"She'll never last here," Chaz predicted to Melody quietly. He took Melody's hand again and gave her a squeeze of reassurance.

Thanks, Melody thought silently. *That means*

that this time I don't have to worry about her stealing you away from me.
I hope.

"Maybe she's just going to make a slow adjustment," Nicole suggested, turning her pillow over and snuggling down under the covers. "That happens sometimes."

"Yeah, and sometimes the Big Guy is just plain wrong," Cisco drawled.

"The Big Guy is never wrong," Nicole stated.

"The girl is a twit. She doesn't belong here. I rest my case," Cisco said.

"We don't get to decide," Melody reminded Cisco. She stared up into the darkness toward the ceiling. It was around eleven-thirty that night, and she and her roommates had just turned the lights out to go to sleep.

But they kept talking about Scarlett Whitmore instead.

Melody recounted the rest of her conversation with Chaz and Scarlett. She told Nicole and Cisco that once they finally got Scarlett to believe that she really was dead and in Teen Heaven, Scarlett had gone from being testy to nasty to downright mean, even accusing Melody and Chaz of having no real feelings of their own when they'd been down to Earth on their mission.

"You're just JD's pawns," Scarlett had sneered. "Don't you see that? You were only nice to me because JD told you to be."

"I tried to tell her what JD says about free will," Melody said softly to her friends. "But—"

"Big shocker, she didn't care," Cisco guessed. "And she's right, in a way. Scarlett Whitmore is obnoxious and hateful. You would not have gone out of your way to be nice to her if you weren't a TA."

"I guess," Melody admitted. "I asked JD about that once. And he told me that people we dislike need our kindness and good deeds even more than people we like."

"Yes, but if you dislike someone you have no desire to be nice to them," Nicole pointed out.

"I know," Melody agreed. "That's the problem."

"I wonder how she got into Teen Heaven," Nicole mused.

"You're the one who says the Big Guy is never wrong," Cisco said.

"He isn't," Nicole replied.

"We'll see," Cisco countered with a yawn. " 'Night, ya'll."

Melody lay on her bed in the dark, as her two friends drifted off to sleep. She could hear their measured breathing, and, though she was exhausted by the day at the beach and the night at Rock Around the Cloud, she couldn't sleep.

Every time she closed her eyes, she saw the vision unfold, over and over again. It was she and Chaz back on Earth, on their mission to Scarlett's school. It was Chaz's first day there, and Scarlett had zeroed in on Chaz like a hawk on its prey.

And there was Scarlett, snaking herself sexily around Chaz, as Melody had looked on helplessly.

She had that same gleam in her eye tonight, Melody thought, as she replayed the conversation in Rock Around the Cloud again and again in her mind.

Scarlett is scared, and Scarlett is mad, Melody thought. *And Scarlett is still having a hard time believing that she's dead.*

But mad and scared and dead, Scarlett was looking at Chaz the same way she had looked at him Down Below. She wanted him.

And there isn't anything I can do about it.

Three

"World's greatest pizza," Jake Silverman exclaimed hungrily, snatching up a huge slice of the super-sized vegetarian three-cheese pie that Cisco had just set down in the middle of the formica cafeteria table.

"You just love to eat," Nicole teased him gently, nudging him in the ribs.

Melody, who was sitting next to Nicole, smiled at her. *It's so sweet that Nicole and Jake met on Earth*, Melody thought. *And when Nicole is around Jake, he gets more ... more playful or something.*

"I am so starved, ya'll," Cisco drawled, reaching for a slice and lifting it to her mouth. "And this is to-die-for."

Everyone at the table—Melody, Cisco, Cisco's new boyfriend Spencer Adams, Nicole, and Jake, laughed.

It was now two days after Scarlett Whitmore's unhappy arrival in Teen Heaven, and the gang was eating lunch together in the fabulous Teen Heaven High School cafeteria. Unlike the usual dreadful high school cafeterias Down Below, the

THHS cafeteria featured expertly prepared gourmet entrees, and everyone always looked forward to lunchtime. It was by far the best meal of the day.

"That was not even an intentional pun," Cisco said through a mouthful of pizza. "But I don't mind taking credit for it, anyway."

"Now that is so . . . so Cisco," Spencer teased, shaking his long hair out of his eyes. Cisco just made a face at him and kept scarfing down her pizza.

"You're not eating," Jake said, cocking his head at the slice in front of Melody.

"Too many fat grams," Melody said with a sigh.

"Mel, this weight thing of yours is not one of your finer qualities," Cisco drawled, polishing off her first slice and reaching for a second.

"I know," Melody agreed. "I'm trying to change." She eyed the pizza longingly. "Why is it that you can still gain weight in heaven, will someone tell me?"

"Just more of those diabolical things we can't understand, I guess," Jake said with a shrug. "Hey, by the way, where's Chaz? He usually eats with us."

"And he can get you to actually eat," Nicole added.

"His schedule was changed," Melody answered softly, taking a sip of the Diet Pepsi she'd picked up. "He eats lunch second period, now."

"When did this happen?" Cisco queried, licking some tomato sauce off her finger.

"This morning," Melody replied. "He's in history class now."

"Ugh," Spencer grimaced. "History. My fave. I don't see why we have to take history. I mean, we're not on Earth anymore, and nothing ever happens here."

"You haven't been here long enough to know that," Nicole pointed out logically.

"So, what's the biggest news since we arrived?" Spencer challenged. "I mean, besides Cisco's latest uni."

Without missing a beat Cisco threw the bread stick she was about to bite into right at Spencer. Spencer caught it in his left hand without moving his arm at all, and everyone laughed.

"Ya'll love my clothes," Cisco drawled. She stood up and spun around, showing off her latest outfit, purchased at her favorite store at Mall Over America, Dead Threads. It consisted of a black pleated mini-jumper over a white t-shirt, with black fishnet stockings and combat boots.

"I do love your clothes," Nicole agreed, "on you. But I would look ridiculous in them."

Melody eyed Nicole's usual conservative, and expensive, outfit, which today was a navy skirt with a white cashmere sweater set.

"Well, it isn't exactly you, I agree," Cisco said. She grinned at Melody. "And we certainly all can't go around dressing like Mel, now can we?"

Melody looked down at her pink denim shorts and cropped denim shirt, over which was a set of pink suspenders. "Does it look okay?" she asked uncertainly.

Cisco groaned. "How can anyone as gorgeous as you be so insecure?"

"I don't know," Melody replied honestly. "I

mean, I don't feel as if I'm gorgeous is what I mean—"

"Hey, that new girl with the blonde hair is in Chaz's history class," Jake interrupted. "What's her name."

"Scah-lett," Cisco said, putting an extra dose of southern syrup on top of her usual Tennessee drawl. "The Evuh Chah-ming Scah-lett Whitmore." She made the end of Scarlett's last name sound like the end of the word "lawnmower."

"She started talking to me after calc," Spencer replied.

"Talking?" Cisco asked.

"Okay, flirting," Spencer admitted.

"Like I care," Cisco snorted. "Scarlett Whitmore is a cross between a pit bull and a gutter snake, so if you want her you can—"

"Yo, yo, chill!" Spencer said with a laugh, holding up his hand. "I didn't say I was interested, I said she was flirting. Big difference."

"So what's her deal, anyway?" Jake asked.

"Did she flirt with you, too?" Nicole asked warily.

"In an obvious and very boring kind of way," Jake said. "I mean, she acts like she's the Big Guy's gift to the male of the species."

"Gag me," Cisco muttered.

"She was terrible to Melody Down Below," Nicole said, sipping her Coke.

"And I failed my mission with her," Melody added. She thought a moment. "I wonder..."

"What?" Jake asked.

"If it's deliberate," Melody said slowly.

"What's deliberate?" Nicole asked her.

A bunch of kids at the next table laughed loudly at something, and Melody waited a moment. "I wonder if it's deliberate that Chaz's schedule got changed," Melody said, her voice trying to belie her own concern, "just when Scarlett Whitmore arrives here, and . . ."

"Oh, Mel, Chaz would never do that," Nicole said staunchly. "He loves you."

"That's not what I meant," Melody said. "I mean do you think JD changed Chaz's schedule so he'd be in classes with Scarlett?"

Everyone was silent for a moment, mulling over that possibility.

"Naaah," Cisco finally said. "JD doesn't manipulate things here in TH. He saves that for our assignments on Earth. I think."

"But you don't know," Nicole pointed out in her clear, precise voice. "None of us knows."

"Do you think if I—" Melody began, finally lifting the slice of pizza to her lips. But she never got to finish her sentence. Or decide whether or not she could risk the fat grams in a slice of triple-cheese pizza. The slice fell to her plate with a gentle little plop, and one mushroom came tumbling off it.

But Melody hadn't dropped her pizza by mistake.

Instead, she'd simply disappeared.

"Melody, Melody, Melody," JD said with a grin. "My most humble apologies. You were about to finally dig into the pizza, which looked major dee-lish."

Melody looked around the Center of Everything, to which she'd magically been transported. In front of her, JD was leaning against one of the see-through crystal pillars that supported the ceiling.

"I wouldn't know," Melody said with a sigh. "It really smelled great, though."

"So, how's tricks?" JD asked, leaning against the wall, his arms folded.

"You should know," Melody said. "You're the only one who can *do* tricks."

"Touché," JD said with a laugh.

"It still seems so strange to me," Melody continued, "this being in one place one minute, and being in a totally different place the next instant."

JD snapped his fingers twice, and Melody's slice of pizza appeared in his hands. He handed it to Melody. "Here. I meant to transport this with you. I must be losing my touch."

"I don't think I'm hungry anymore," Melody said, handing the slice back to JD. "Thanks, anyway."

JD shook his head. "I am not appreciated around here at all." He took a huge bite out of the slice of pizza. "Mmmm, great."

"JD, I don't think you blipped me here to tell me that the cafeteria makes great pizza," Melody guessed.

JD took a couple more satisfying bites before he turned his attention back to Melody, who just stood there before him, watching.

"Oh!" JD said finally. "Where are my manners? Please sit down." He motioned Melody over to the front row of seats in the Center of

Everything, directly in front of the floor-to-ceiling EarthScope. Melody went and sat in one of the plush theater seats.

"Mission time," JD said.

"I had that feeling when you beamed me here," Melody said. "But why now?" Melody asked him. "Scarlett is here and Chaz is—"

"You know what I always say," JD said cheerfully, "never hurry, never worry! Besides, there's no time like the present."

"But Scarlett Whitmore just—"

"Hey babe," JD said, "you should be happy you're going Down Below. That girl is bad news."

"I know, JD," Melody said, "that's why I'm so concerned about her and—"

"You want to stay here and hang out with Scarlett?" JD asked incredulously.

Melody shook her head.

"So, what's the prob, babe?" JD asked, sitting down next to Melody.

How can I really tell him what I want? she thought. *I don't want to leave Scarlett up here with Chaz alone. I saw that look in her eyes in the cafe. She hates me. And she wants him.*

She'll do anything to hurt me if she can.

But I can't tell JD that. He'll think I'm a bad Teen Angel.

Well, maybe I am.

"Nothing," Melody finally said. "No problem."

"Cool," JD said easily. "Go Down Below, earn some quick Angel Points, come back—who knows? Maybe she'll be history by then."

"History?" Melody asked, her eyes huge. "You mean she might go to Deep—"

"Ours is not to wonder why, babe," JD said philosophically.

"But if she ended up in . . . you know," Melody said, unable to actually bring herself to say it out loud, "it would be my fault! I failed with her on my mission, and—"

"Mel, sometimes you're a wee bit too hard on yourself," JD said. He stood up and stretched. "Man, I gotta get some exercise. I been working too hard." He straightened out a crick in his back and turned back to Melody. "Where was I? Oh, yeah, your mission."

He snapped his fingers. Instantly, the lights in the Center of Everything glowed purple, then a floor-to-ceiling picture illuminated on the screen.

It was a big group of kids—they looked to Melody to range in age from three to six—all playing, screaming, yelling, and running around together.

"Preschool?" Melody asked, her voice catching in her throat. She'd never had a lot of experience with young kids—all her modeling jobs meant that she never had to work as a baby-sitter or camp counselor or anything ordinary like that. And her younger brother Down Below was living with her father.

Or so her mother had told her. She'd never actually met either her father or her brother, not that she could recall.

"Daycare," JD said, shaking his head ruefully. "Bad deal. They hardly pay the workers there anything."

"But what about the children? Don't they—"

JD cut her off with a wave of his hand, as the camera came in tight on a young African-

American woman who looked to be about twenty years old. Her hair was out of place, her shirt had come out of the jeans she was wearing. She looked totally and completely harried.

Not that I blame her, Melody thought quickly, as she saw the woman go over and comfort a crying little boy. The din in the daycare was deafening. *That place is complete bedlam!*

"Like I said," JD repeated, "she's your mission."

Melody gulped.

"Don't worry," JD assured her, snapping off the Earthscope, "she's no Scarlett Whitmore. This one's a piece of cake."

Melody smiled noncommittally, as JD handed her the by-now-familiar manila dossier that contained all the information that she would need about her mission.

"What's her name?" Melody asked.

"It's in there," JD replied, indicating the dossier. "And—"

JD cocked suddenly his head, as if someone was speaking to him.

"Uh huh," he said. "Uh huh. Okay, you got it, Bossman. Be there in a sec."

The Big Guy, Melody thought. *The Big Guy is talking to him.*

"But—"

"I'm summoned," JD said quickly. "And when the Big Guy calls, I'm outta here."

"But can you actually talk to Him?" Melody asked, wonder in her voice.

"Of course," JD answered.

"But do you see Him?" Melody persisted. "Because I heard that—"

"Can't answer that now," JD replied, a grin crossing his face. "Maybe one day you'll know. Later!"

Then JD snapped his fingers, and he was gone. Melody sighed, and opened the thin manila envelope JD had handed her. She started to read the short memo that was inside. Per usual, it had JD's trademark fancy letterhead at the top.

To: Melody Monroe
From: JD
Subject: Mission #2 for you

This one is a piece of cake. You're going to be going to western Massachusetts, to a little town called Stockbridge. It's pretty. Bring your camera. Your mission is that woman you saw on the EarthScope. Her name is Tarshea Williams. She's twenty years old, she's got a kid, and she doesn't have it easy.

She works at the Happy Days Daycare Center in Stockbridge five days a week. And she's been studying at night on her own to get her high school diploma, since she dropped out of school when she was fifteen.

How's that for initiative? I gotta tell ya, babe, the Big Guy is really proud of her, for the responsibility she's showing now.

Now, her General Equivalency Degree test is coming up, and she needs three solid days to prepare.

Oh my God, Melody thought quickly. *He doesn't want me to be her tutor, does he? Because I can barely do long division! In fact, I was a terrible student!*

She took a deep breath and willed herself not to freak herself out for nothing.

Melody read on.

Tarshea has a problem. There's a labor shortage in Stockbridge, and Happy Days hasn't been able to find anyone to replace her. So they don't want to give her the time off to take her test.

That's where you come in. You're going to be her temporary replacement. It's all set. You'll be staying at a famous old inn in Stockbridge just down the street from Happy Days. You're gonna be working twelve hours a day at the daycare center. And you're gonna be great. I know it.

Have fun.

And then, at the bottom of the memo was JD's huge signature. Under it was a handwritten postscript.

P.S. Oh yeah. Sorry that I broke into your lunch. Now that you're finished reading this, go back and enjoy the rest of it.

Melody no sooner read these words than she felt the weirdest sensation come over her body. She closed her eyes because she felt a little dizzy.

When she opened them, she was again sitting in the cafeteria, right between Cisco and Nicole, just as she had been fifteen minutes before.

". . . that's not a guy, it's a girl!" Jake finished, and everyone at the table laughed their heads off.

Except Melody. She just sat there in a daze.

"Want to hear Jake's joke?" Spencer asked.

"How long was I gone?" Melody asked.

"Maybe two minutes," Cisco said. "JD does some kind of weird time thing when he beams you out. I assume it was JD who beamed you out, right?"

"Right," Melody agreed.

"So, what's up?" Cisco asked, reaching for her Coke.

"I just got my second mission Down Below," Melody reported.

"Cool," Spencer said enthusiastically.

"Are you going to have time to say good-bye to Chaz before you go?" Nicole asked.

"I don't know," Melody replied, gulping hard. "But here's what I do know. I'm going to be Down Below. And Scarlett Whitmore is going to be up here with Chaz. And there is absolutely nothing that I can do about it."

Four

It was a half hour later, and the three girls were still sitting in the cafeteria talking. A whole new group of kids had come in for lunch, and Jake and Spencer had gone outside to shoot hoops.

"I still say you should have just told JD how concerned you are about Scarlett and Chaz," Nicole maintained for the fourth time.

"But I'm supposed to be this Teen Angel!" Melody cried. "An angel wouldn't have such an unangelic thought!" She fiddled with the straw in her soda, which was now lukewarm. "Let's face it. At any moment JD could beam me out of here like that," she snapped her fingers.

"It's the physics of it that bothers me," Nicole said thoughtfully.

"Of my Earth mission?" Melody asked, confused.

"Physics, gag me with a harp," Cisco grumbled. "A year of high school torture. Never thought I'd ever use it in my life. Guess what?"

"What?" Melody asked.

"I was right."

"What I mean is, how does JD move bodies around in space the way he does? Do we move molecule by molecule, or—"

"Nicole," Cisco interrupted. "Kindly hush up. We're trying to help Mel here, not talk about physics."

"Sorry," Nicole said with a shrug. She looked up at the clock, which featured angel wings that pointed to the numbers. There were just five minutes left before the end of lunch period.

"So, listen," Cisco said, "we've been talking so much about this deal with Scarlett that you haven't even told us what your mission is. Destination?"

Melody reached for a grape from the bowl of fruit that was in the middle of the table. "Someplace in Massachusetts. It doesn't sound very difficult," she said quietly. "I'm going to be working for a few days in a daycare center."

"Gawd," Cisco said, putting both her hands on her face and looking out through the spread-out fingers. "Not hard? A daycare center? Not *hard?* All those screaming little kids barfing on each other? Better you than me."

"But I like little kids," Melody said softly. "Someday I hope to have a whole bunch of kids of my own and—"

She stopped, realizing what she had just said. "I mean," she finally continued, "I used to hope to have a whole bunch of kids . . ."

Nicole touched Melody's hand softly. "It's okay, Mel."

Melody tried to smile. "Maybe once we get to Ultimate Heaven we get to get married and have a family!"

"Maybe," Cisco said. "Not that I'm pining for marriage, myself."

Nicole rubbed a spot on the table with her index finger and sighed. "It's so bizarre, isn't it. I mean, love used to lead to marriage and family—at least some day. But now . . ."

"Now we just don't know," Cisco said.

"Do you think JD would tell us if we asked him?" Melody wondered.

Nicole tried to smile, but there were tears in her eyes. "But what if we ask and we get an answer we don't want to hear?"

Melody heard Cisco catch her breath, and turned to her left to look at her friend.

There's a tear in Cisco's eye, too, Melody realized.

"I'm so sorry," Melody said quietly. "I didn't mean to—"

Cisco interrupted her. "It's okay," but her voice was a little choked up. "I mean, it's not your fault we're here, is it?" She tried to smile. "Anyway, my kid sister was always the one who wanted to get married and have a family, not me."

"What's her name again?" Nicole asked.

"Shelby," Cisco said. "It's just that . . . well, I've been thinking about Shelby a lot lately."

"I've been thinking about my brother and sister, too," Nicole admitted. "I wonder if they think about me?"

"Of course they do," Cisco said. "You're their sister! Anyway, maybe you'll see them on a mission sometime. Or go look at them on the EarthScope."

"That costs thousands of Angel Points," Nicole pointed out. "Which I do not have to spare, since I've only done one mission so far, unfortunately."

As the angel's wings moved to one o'clock, a trill on a harp signaled the end of their lunch period. Since the periods were staggered, about half the kids in the cafeteria got up, the others just kept right on eating.

Melody and her friends got up, too.

"Good luck, Mel," Nicole said sincerely, turning to her friend. "If we don't see you before you go." She gave Melody a quick hug.

Cisco threw her arms around Melody. "Have fun with the kiddies," she said slyly. "I hope you've had chicken pox already."

A whole bunch of very hungry Teen Heaven High School students came through the cafeteria doors, making a beeline for the food line. Melody had to edge Cisco out of the way in order for them to pass by unimpeded.

"I'll try," Melody answered. "I don't even know when I'm going down . . ." Suddenly, Melody started to get that familiar shimmering sensation.

"Mel?" Nicole asked. "You have a funny look on your face."

"Uh, I have a feeling I do know when I'm going to get beamed down," Melody said. "Now." She gave her friends a panicked look. "I failed at my last mission, what if I—"

"You can do it, Melody!" Nicole said. "We know you can do it!"

"And we'll keep Scarlett on a leash while you're gone," Cisco promised. "She won't even get to breathe the same air as Chaz."

"You guys are the best," Melody said gratefully. "Make sure Ruffy isn't too lonely, and—"

Melody's voice trailed away as she felt her body continue to dematerialize. The whole world looked topsy-turvy and out-of-whack.

Then Melody got a sickening feeling in her stomach, like she was about to throw up.

And it wasn't the fact that she was in the throes of being transported down to Earth that caused her to feel nauseous. It was the last thing she saw before she disappeared completely.

Chaz was walking into the cafeteria.

And Scarlett Whitmore was walking right by his side, laughing gaily, and tucking her arm into his.

"Hi!"

Melody looked up at the young woman speaking to her, and blinked a couple of time.

"Hi!" the woman repeated. "Can I get you something? Juice? Coffee? Tea?"

"Huh?" Melody mumbled, opening her eyes wide, now.

Melody was sitting again, but instead of being in the Teen Heaven High School cafeteria, she was now in a old white wicker rocking chair, on the crowded front porch of an old inn. To her left and to her right, instead of her buds from Teen Heaven, were all manner of people and tourists, also rocking back in forth in chairs, and either reading, snoozing, or engaging in animated conversation.

The air was warm, but there was more than a hint of autumn in the gentle breeze that swirled around the porch. Melody could see that all the stately trees that lined the street in front of her were in the midst of their blazing fall colors—the brightest reds and yellows she'd ever seen before.

I must be in Stockbridge, Massachusetts, Melody realized. *And it's the middle of the autumn here. It is unbelievably beautiful!*

And Chaz was walking into the cafeteria with Scarlett Whitmore just as I was leaving. So much for Cisco keeping her away from him.

Melody's heart sank quickly.

"So, can I get you anything?" the young waitress asked Melody again, pushing her windblown short blonde hair out of her eyes. She wore a name tag on her blue sweater that read: "Meredith, Monument Mountain High School, Great Barrington, Mass."

"A Diet Coke, please." Melody said, "Meredith."

"Will this be a room charge?" the waitress asked, smiling again.

Melody was stumped. *A room charge? I don't know what room I'm in,* she thought. *Or even if I'm staying here at this inn!*

Then Meredith laughed. "I am so blind," she giggled. "Your key with your number on it is right on the table in front of you. You're in room twenty."

"Room twenty," Melody replied. "That's right."

How did that key get there? Melody asked herself. *And when did I check in?*

Meredith's voice dropped to a whisper. "Some people say that room's haunted."

"Oh, really," Melody said with a smile.

Meredith nodded, her eyes wide. "Some big violinist with the Boston Symphony killed himself in that room," Meredith confided. "They say sometimes you can still hear him play. But I've never seen the ghost myself."

"I'll watch for him. Or listen," Melody promised.

"Some guests don't want to stay in that room," Meredith confided. "On the other hand, some people call up way ahead of time and request it!"

"Well, I guess I just lucked into it," Melody said.

Meredith laughed. "Listen, I hope you don't mind my saying this, but has anyone ever told you you look just like—"

"Marilyn Monroe," Melody put in. "I know."

"I was going to say Pamela Anderson," Meredith said. "You know, the one who married that rock star—"

Melody smiled. "Well, I'm not married at all." *And I probably will never get to be married, either,* she added in her own mind.

"Okay, one Diet Coke coming right up." Meredith said, walking away.

She's nice, Melody thought. *Really nice. I would have liked to have had a friend like that in high school.*

Melody looked around, taking stock of her surroundings. She was sitting on the front porch of someplace called the Red Lion Inn, where she apparently was also staying, in the apparently infamous room 20. She could tell from a sign in front of the inn that it had been built sometime around the American Revolution—it was *that* old.

In front of her, from left to right, ran Stockbridge's Main Street. At the moment, it was full of cars and even the stray tourist bus, and there was an older, overweight policeman standing at the intersection to her left, directing traffic.

The houses and low-slung buildings on the street were all quaint, and many of them, Melody could see, even had pumpkins and Indian corn near their front doors.

It's so beautiful here, Melody thought. *It looks like a postcard, or those Norman Rockwell paintings that Chaz was showing me at school.*

Melody looked down at the white wicker table that held her room key, and saw that her mission folder was right beside her key. She picked it up and idly leafed through it.

There's a map that shows where Happy Days Daycare is, Melody mused, *and it looks like it's right down the street from here. And there's a post-it note on the map that says I'm supposed to report there at eight A.M. tomorrow.*

"One Diet Coke!" chimed Meredith, pulling Melody's attention away from her folder. The waitress set the soda down on the wicker table.

"Thanks," Melody said gratefully, reaching down for the soda, and bringing it to her lips for a long sip.

Meredith handed Melody the bill, and Melody signed it and handed it back to her.

"So, where are you from?" Meredith asked.

"Far away," Melody said honestly. "I was born in Detroit. You know, this town is so gor-

43

geous. It looks like it could be in a painting or something."

Meredith laughed. "It *has* been in paintings," she told Melody. "Norman Rockwell lived here. His museum is here. Didn't you read the guidebook in your room?"

Melody shook her head no.

"Well, it's worth checking out," Meredith said.

"I will," Melody promised. "And I'll definitely go to the museum."

Chaz will love that I went to an art museum myself, Melody thought happily, recalling how he had taken her to the very first art museum she had ever been to.

Chaz.

Melody's stomach sank again, as she recalled the image of Chaz and Scarlett Whitmore walking into the Teen Heaven High School cafeteria together just before she was sent down on this mission.

I can't think about that now, she told herself. *I'm a Teen Angel with a mission.*

She forced her mind back to her job. "Meredith, do you know what direction Happy Days Daycare Center is?"

Meredith took her pencil and pointed to the right. "Right down there," she said. "Make a right, and it's just beyond the post office. How come?"

"Oh, I have an appointment there tomorrow," Melody said nonchalantly.

"Well, if you see a little girl who looks just like me," Meredith said, grinning, "it's my sister Emily."

"You have a sister at Happy Days?" Melody asked.

"Yep," Meredith answered. "Eight-thirty to five, five days a week, so mom can work and I can go to school."

"Where's your dad? Or is that too personal—"

"It's okay," Meredith said with a shrug. "The great Daddy Beyond," she intoned.

"I'm sorry to hear that he's dead," Melody said solemnly.

"Oh, he's not dead—at least not that I know of," Meredith said. "He's just beyond us. Where daddies go when they don't want to pay child support. So what's up with you and the daycare center?"

"Actually," Melody answered, "I'm working there for a few days. As a favor."

"Oh, great!" Meredith said. "Emily will love you. You look like her favorite Barbie doll! I'll tell her all about you tonight."

"How old is she?" Melody asked.

"Five," Meredith answered. "Going on twenty-five. Don't get too close to her, she's in her kung fu stage."

A customer at the other end of the porch gestured wildly with his right arm, trying to get Meredith's attention. "Miss! Miss! I need some service!"

"Be right there, sir!" Meredith called to him. "Some of these people are so rude," she whispered to Melody. "So, what's your name? So I can tell Emily."

"Melody," Melody said. "Melody Monroe."

Meredith laughed. "Right," she said. "You might as well tell me it's Penelope Anderson and you're Pamela Anderson's sister."

"It's my real name," Melody said. "Honest."

"Well, whatever," Meredith said breezily. "I still like you. So, see you soon, I hope!" She headed for the customer, who was now scowling in her direction.

I hope Emily takes after her sister, Melody thought, as she reached for her Diet Coke and took another big sip.

And I hope my room isn't really haunted!

Five

RAP! RAP! RAP!

Melody banged the old-fashioned door knocker hard against the big wooden front door of the Happy Days Daycare Center, for the second time. The first time she'd tried, just a few moments earlier, there'd been no answer at all.

She looked down to check her watch again, even though she knew perfectly well what time it was.

Exactly 7:30 A.M. Work started at eight.

I'm sure I'm on time, Melody thought. *Or else JD has made his very first mistake!*

It was the next morning, and Melody had set the radio alarm in room 20 for six o'clock in the morning, to be absolutely certain that she'd have enough to time to dress and eat before leaving for the daycare center.

The evening before, in the small closet in room 20, she'd found a suitcase that was full of her favorite clothes from Teen Heaven. And even though she had no idea how JD had arranged for that suitcase to get there, she'd gratefully picked out a pair of white jeans and a pink and white t-shirt to wear to her first day on the job.

After that, she'd spent the entire evening back out in her white rocker on the Red Lion Inn's front porch, drinking hot chocolate, and watching the weekend visitors' cars stream out of Stockbridge, en route to their real homes in and around New York City, three tiring hours away.

By nine o'clock at night, the little town was quiet and still. And except for some odd cackling laughter she'd heard from someplace just after she'd entered her room, and a couple of souped-up cars that had skidded noisily down Main Street just before she turned off her antique bedside lamp, Stockbridge had stayed peaceful and quiet.

No haunting in her room.

No ghosts.

Melody reached for the door knocker a third time.

I hope I haven't made a mistake. I'm sure this is exactly when JD told me that I'd have to start today. So why isn't anyone—

The front door swung open.

There, in front of her, stood Tarshea Williams, the subject of her mission, a quizzical look on her face.

Melody quickly took in her very slim, five-foot-five figure with dark, chocolately skin, her very short haircut, her long, graceful neck, her huge dark eyes. Early as it was in the morning, and even dressed as casually as she was, in worn sneakers, jeans, and a simple red-and-blue t-shirt, Tarshea looked, somehow, elegant. Quite a bit different from the harried-looking worker

Melody had watched with JD on the EarthScope.

"May I help you?" Tarshea asked, her voice betraying a hint of a lilting accent that Melody couldn't place.

"I'm Melody Monroe," Melody said politely. "And you're Tarshea, right?"

Tarshea's eyes suddenly narrowed, and her forehead furrowed suspiciously.

Oh no, Melody thought, her stomach turning over in a panic. *I can't believe I just said that. What a goof! I'm sure she's wondering how in the world I would know her name! And the answer is, I wouldn't!*

"Have we met?" Tarshea asked warily.

"Why, no, uh—" Melody sputtered, "I don't think we've ever—"

"Then, how do you know my name?" Tarshea demanded, her hands on her hips.

"I . . . I met a girl at the Red Lion Inn whose sister Emily goes here," Melody improvised quickly. "She told me all about you—what you looked like—said how great you were with Emily."

"What's the girl's name?" Tarshea queried, no trust at all in her voice.

"The girl?" Melody asked.

Oh gosh. I can't remember her name.

"It's, uh . . . Mol—Meredith!" Melody answered, suddenly remembering Meredith's nameplate. "She lives around here. She's a waitress at the Red Lion Inn, part-time."

Tarshea's face softened. "That's right," she said, in that same lilting accent. "We have Emily here. I have met Meredith. They are both wonderful."

Melody breathed a quick sigh of relief.

"I hope you'll forgive me for being so suspicious," Tarshea continued in her melodious, lilting accent, "but we have to be very careful—for the sake of the children."

"I understand," Melody said, nodding.

"Now," Tarshea said hurriedly, "how can I help you? Quickly, because I am awaiting my temporary replacement here. I must orient her when she comes."

"I'm her," Melody said softly.

"You?" Tarshea laughed. "I don't think so. You are too beautiful to work in a daycare center."

"So are you," Melody said honestly.

Tarshea's face lit up at the compliment, then she threw her head back and laughed. "You wouldn't think so when I've got modeling clay in my hair and some child has spilled fruit juice on my shirt. So who are you, really?" Tarshea asked again, with a broad smile. "You don't work here."

"My name is Melody Monroe," Melody said. "I understand that you're taking a few days off. I'm your replacement. Really. An agency sent me."

That's true, Melody thought. *In a way.*

Tarshea gave Melody a wry grin. "So you may be," she said, her voice soft and lilting. "I hope very much you like the children! One thing is for sure."

"What's that?" Melody asked.

"You'll find out!"

"Okay, Melody," Tarshea said. "I'm off now. You remember everything?"

Tarshea and Melody stood together right at the front door to Happy Days, exactly where they'd met a half-hour before.

"I hope so," Melody said nervously, looking down at the school notebook she'd used to take notes on her duties. Her neat, small handwriting filled several pages.

"I hope so, too," Tarshea smiled. "Mrs. Plant and Mrs. Driver will be here in ten minutes. The children start arriving at eight-thirty."

"Okay," Melody said, dubiously considering her notes, "I suppose I'm ready. I hope!"

"I'm off, then," Tarshea said. "Good luck." She reached her hand out for Melody's and gave it a gentle squeeze.

"Thanks," Melody said. "Oh, Tarshea?"

"Yeah?" Tarshea replied. It sounded like she was saying the word "yah."

"I love your accent," Melody said honestly. "It's beautiful. Where are you from?"

Tarshea sighed. "Jamaica," she answered. "A beautiful island in the Caribbean. My mother and sister came here with me when I was fifteen. My sister was just a baby."

"That's all there is in your family?" Melody asked, remembering what JD had written in her memo about Tarshea having a child, but not wanting to give that fact away to her new friend.

"That's all, sister," Tarshea answered.

"Oh," Melody replied, trying to hide her puzzlement. She was sure that JD had told her that Tarshea had a child.

Why is she lying to me? Melody wondered.

"This is your last chance to ask me questions,"

Tarshea said, fitting her blue backpack on to her back. "So speak up now."

"I probably should have a million, but I can't think of any," Melody admitted. "I guess I'll see you in three days or so."

"That's right," Tarshea agreed, edging toward the door. "Good luck, Melody."

She turned and headed down the flagstone walkway that led around the daycare center to a small parking lot. Melody watched her—Tarshea walked as elegantly as she looked.

Then, halfway down the walkway, Tarshea stopped, and turned around, to see if Melody was still watching her.

She was.

"It's just my sister and me, now, Melody Monroe," Tarshea said. "My mother . . . she died of . . . she died. So it means a lot to me that you're working here now, so I can prepare for my school test. Even if I don't know who really sent you."

Melody couldn't think of an answer before Tarshea had turned around again and headed for the small parking lot. A few moments later, Tarshea pull out of the driveway in a beat-up old station wagon.

JD was right. She does have a little girl, Melody realized, *but the little girl isn't her daughter. It's her sister. So she wasn't lying to me after all.*

Tarshea waved to Melody as her car sped by, and then Melody was once more alone, to face the kiddie army that was due to arrive any minute.

Ready or not.

* * *

"Melody, play with me!"
"No, me!"
"No, me!"
"No, I asked her first!"
"Please?"
"Pretty please?"
"Pretty please with sugar on top?"
"Shut up, you doody-bomb! I asked first!"

Melody took a deep breath, and snuck a glance at the clock on the wall. It was only eleven. Which meant that she had been working at Happy Days Daycare Center for exactly two and one half hours.

Which felt like two and a half years.

Her right shin hurt from where some little boy named Lance—who had obviously been spending too much time watching certain shows on television—had delivered a vicious spinning karate kick to it.

I never thought a child could kick so hard, Melody thought ruefully, feeling her shin throb. *He's only three years old!*

Her back hurt, because she had spent the better part of the morning carrying around a four-year-old girl named Lauren, who had started crying the minute she'd learned that Melody was Tarshea's replacement, and who could not seem to grasp the concept that Melody was only Tarshea's *temporary* replacement and that Tarshea was going to be back at work in just a few days.

The only thing that would keep Lauren from crying was if Melody carried her in her arms. Which is exactly what Melody did.

And the only reason that I'm not carrying her now, Melody thought, *is that Lauren got so tired from crying that she had to take a nap. I feel bad for her, I really do, but I also feel bad for me.*

Her ears hurt, because a group of the oldest kids, age five, had all been singing a version of a song called "The Song That Never Ends," which they had also learned from a television show. The song, which Melody had never heard before, did not have an actual ending but just went on and on and on. And on.

The five-year-olds were currently proving that the song could last at least forty-five minutes.

There was no end in sight.

All of which was combining to give Melody a very earthly splitting headache.

And it was only eleven o'clock in the morning.

Mrs. Plant and Mrs. Driver can't even help me, Melody ruminated, *because they're outside with an even bigger group of kids. It's up to me in here, ready or not. And Tarshea, whatever they were paying you, it's not enough!*

Then Melody remembered something. She quickly consulted her notebook to confirm her thought.

"Hey kids," she called out, "it's eleven o'clock. Do you know what time that is?"

"Eleven o'clock!" one of the kids sang out.

"You're so stupid, you doody-bomb," sneered freckle-faced Duane, who Melody had secretly nicknamed the Doody-Bomb Kid, since it was the all-purpose insult he used on everyone.

"Time for the song that never ends!" another kid yelled.

"At Happy Days we all are friends! ... " A group of about five kids started singing—no, screaming—joining the group that had been singing it for the last forty-five minutes.

"Time for Melody to play with me!"

"No, me!"

"No, me!"

"No, I asked her first!"

"Please?"

"Pretty please?"

"Pretty please with sugar on top?"

"Shut up, you doody-bomb, I asked her first!"

Melody closed her eyes. *Did I say I was sad because I'll never get to have children? I may have to rethink that position . . .*

She took a deep breath and forced herself to be reasonable and cheerful. "Hey, everyone it's . . . morning snack time!"

"YEEEEAH!"

The kids were going wild, but Melody heaved a sigh of relief. Because the singing/screaming group had actually stopped singing/screaming.

At that moment, a bell clanged from the kitchen area.

Mrs. Plant and Mrs. Driver, Melody thought. *To the rescue. Thank you.*

Another huge cheer went up from the group of kids, who wasted no time in running, en masse, for the small Happy Days kitchen.

One little girl, who Melody had noticed earlier playing quietly by herself with a big stack of building blocks, didn't run over to the kitchen. Instead, she neatly gathered up all her blocks, put them away in their box, and only then started walking to the kitchen.

Melody fell in next to her.

"You're very neat," Melody told the little girl, who looked to be about five years old. She was wearing cute yellow bib overalls with a little denim shirt, and had short blonde hair and the sweetest blue eyes that Melody had ever seen.

"Thank you," the girl said politely, stopping to gaze up at Melody.

"What's your name?" Melody asked her.

"I'm Emily Elizabeth Macklin," the girl said, just as politely. "My phone number is 885-4323."

Melody was taken aback for a moment, and then laughed.

Of course, she thought. *She sees me as an authority figure, and her parents taught her to give her phone number to authority figures.*

"Emily," Melody repeated, thinking of something. "Do you have an older sister?"

"Meredith," Emily confirmed. "Do you know my sister?"

"I met her yesterday," Melody told the little girl. "I'm staying at the Red Lion Inn."

"Isn't my sister pretty?" Emily asked.

"Very," Melody agreed.

"You're pretty, too," Emily said shyly. She snuck her tiny hand into Melody's. "You look like my favorite Barbie doll!"

Melody's heart turned over, and she felt a lump come to her throat. *I think I just changed my mind again,* she thought to herself. *I can't believe that I'll never have a little girl like this of my own ...*

"So you want me to show you where to go for snacks?" Emily asked Melody politely, gazing up at her.

"Sure," Melody agreed. "You lead the way."

But just as Melody took a step forward, a

strange sensation came over her. She blinked. And blinked again.

And when she opened her eyes, what she saw made her scream louder than she'd ever screamed before in her life.

Or her death.

Six

"AAAARRRRGH!"

Melody's scream caught in her throat, like a hand was suddenly clamping around it.

A hurricane-force wind tore past her, turning her long, blonde hair into a bird's nest of tangles and knots.

In front of her was only blackness.

And the roller-coaster car Melody was now sitting in continued its plunge down the steepest incline Melody had ever seen.

Roller coaster??

Melody screamed again.

"AAAARGH!"

The scream was swallowed up by the rushing wind.

How did I get here? Melody managed to think, pushing her terror aside. *One minute I was in Happy Days Daycare Center, the next minute I'm ...*

JD.

JD must have beamed me back up to Teen Heaven.

But I didn't know that Teen Heaven had a roller coaster. No one told me about it.

So here I am. I hate roller coasters. I'm scared to death of roller coasters. So why am I all alone in the very first car?

The roller coaster slowed momentarily, as it started to chug its way up an enormous incline, which Melody quickly realized was going to give way to another heart-stopping plunge.

Melody, gripping the safety bar of her rollercoaster car, glanced quickly to her left and to her right.

And what she saw, stunned her.

It was the biggest amusement park she'd ever seen, lit up in spectacular fashion because it was nighttime. Back when she was a girl, her mother had taken her once on a driving vacation to Disneyworld, in Florida. And she had been amazed and delighted by it.

It was the only family vacation we ever took, Melody recalled. *She always said we couldn't afford it. And she always said that I couldn't afford to slack off on my career by being out of town, except for that one time* ...

Melody gazed out at the amusement park below her. It was so huge that in comparison Disneyworld looked like the assortment of rides at a rural county fair.

This amusement park seemed literally to stretch from horizon to horizon, in the most spectacular seas of lights and multicolored lasers she'd ever seen.

Where am I? Melody thought again. *Because JD never told any of us about this place.*

And then a terrible thought hit Melody in the pit of her stomach.

Oh no. I hope this isn't Deep Six. And that my punishment is to ride this roller coaster over and over and over again, each time as if it was my first ride, being scared to death over and over again. Because I don't think that I could stand that. Please, no, please—

"Hey Mel!"

Is someone calling me? Or am I imagining it? Melody wondered, as the car climbed slowly to the pinnacle of the track.

"Hey, Melody!"

Melody turned her head completely around, her hands still gripping the safety bar so firmly that her knuckles were snow-white.

"AAAARGH!"

Melody screamed as the train of roller-coaster cars hit the top of the incline, and then plunged down the track toward the ground with sickening speed.

Please stop please stop please stop, Melody prayed, *please pretty please . . .*

And Melody's prayers were answered. The roller coaster finally slowed to a stop, but not before snaking through a series of three S turns so sharp and abrupt that Melody was thrown from side to side in her car.

Finally, it was over. The safety bar on the car snapped up, an exit ramp magically appeared by her car, and Melody was free to go.

"THANK YOU FOR RIDING THE ANGEL-MAKER," a mechanical voice intoned. "NEXT RIDE BEGINS IN EXACTLY FIVE MINUTES.

SHOULD YOU CHOOSE TO EXIT, PLEASE DO SO NOW."

I don't think I can move, Melody thought, letting her head fall back against the back of her seat. *Of course, if I don't move, I'm going to have to do this all over again.*

That thought was enough to get her to sprint from the car.

"Hey, Melody!"

Cisco and Nicole came running up the exit ramp toward her car, both of them grinning broadly.

"Melody!" Nicole cried. "How did you get here?"

"You're done with your mission?" Cisco asked her.

Melody just stood there, a sick look on her face. "That roller coaster—"

"It's the coolest, isn't it?" Cisco cried. "I rode it six times already!"

"I hate roller coasters," Melody managed to say.

"She *is* kind of white," Nicole told Cisco.

Her two friends reached for Melody to help steady her, and they led her over to a bench painted sky blue, with fluffy white clouds scattered around it.

"Thanks," Melody said gratefully.

"Welcome back," Cisco told her friend, plopping down next to her. "Is your mission over?"

"I don't know," Melody confessed. "I mean, one minute I was in the daycare center holding Emily Macklin's little hand, and the next minute, poof!"

"The same thing happened to me," Nicole reminded Melody, "on my mission. Then, JD sent me right back to where I was. And it was like no time had passed."

"It must have been intense Down Below," Cisco said, eyeing Melody's clothes.

"THE ANGEL-MAKER LEAVES IN TWO MINUTES," the mechanical voice intoned. To the girls' left, as they walked, a long line of teenagers snaked their way toward the roller-coaster entrance.

"What do you mean?" Melody asked. "Did you see me on the EarthScope?"

Cisco laughed. "Not hardly. Have you looked in a mirror lately?"

Melody shook her head. "I've been busy with the children," she confessed. "Really, really, really busy. All morning. And it felt like an eternity."

Cisco reached out her right hand toward Melody's face, and plucked away a lollipop that was stuck to Melody's hair. She presented it to her friend, and Nicole laughed out loud.

"A souvenir from one of your little darlings," Cisco quipped.

"Oh, gross," Melody breathed, pitching the pop toward the nearby trash can.

"You look like you're wearing the morning's work," Nicole said.

Melody looked down at herself, and saw that Nicole was absolutely right. On her pink shirt was an assortment of Play-Doh, Silly Putty, and toddler drool. And her white jeans were marked with stray lines of different colors of crayons, and what she suspected might be a disgusting gift from The Doody-Bomb Kid.

"I should have worn armor to work," Melody said.

"Or at least something that doesn't show dirt," Nicole pointed out.

"Where are we, anyway?" Melody asked, craning her neck around.

"TeenHeavenWorld," Nicole responded. "And the answer to your next question is no, we didn't know it was here, either."

"JD brought all of Teen Heaven," Cisco reported, "because he was happy with how we all did in school this week. Even me, believe it or not."

"Or more specifically, *our* Teen Heaven," Nicole specified.

"What does that mean?" Melody asked.

Nicole thrust a glossy, full-cover guidebook with the word TeenHeavenWorld! on the cover into Melody's hand, and Melody leafed through it quickly.

So TeenHeavenWorld is the hugest amusement park ever built, Melody read. *It has all the rides from all the world's greatest parks, plus some rides that don't even exist Down Below. And it's not just for our Teen Heaven, but for the Teen Heavens for French kids, and Russian kids, and Mexican kids, and—*

As if to underscore this last point, a big group of Asian teens, although they were dressed in very cool, typically American clothes, barreled by, laughing and shouting ... and talking happily and hurriedly in Japanese.

"So ours isn't the only Teen Heaven," Melody

said with wonder, taking in the significance of what she had just read.

"Apparently not," Nicole replied, raising her voice a notch, as a rock 'n' roll band had just started playing somewhere off in the distance. "Apparently, there are lots of Teen Heavens, for kids from different countries, which just makes sense because—"

Cisco interrupted her. "Uh, not to interrupt or anything," she began.

"But you just did interrupt," Nicole said seriously.

Cisco laughed. "You slay me, Nicole. What I was going to say is, it's Saturday night, and the park closes at midnight. Which means we only have—"

Melody shook her head. "Did you say it's Saturday night?"

"Of course," Nicole said. "Why?"

"Because I left here on a Tuesday," Melody said, trying to figure it out as she spoke. "And I was Down Below for two days. Which means it should be—"

"Thursday," Nicole completed her sentence for her. "But it's not. My physics teacher says that time is not finite; JD—or should I say the JD working for the Big Guy—can expand, shrink, change it at will. You see, JD—"

Cisco put her hands playfully around Nicole's neck. "No more school! And that's an order!"

"You're right," Nicole decided, nodding emphatically.

"Hey!" Melody said. "I just thought of something. If everyone's here, then Chaz is here too, right?"

"Right," Cisco said. Melody saw Cisco and Nicole look at each other quickly.

"What?" Melody asked.

"What-what?" Nicole said.

"That look," Melody explained. "Is something wrong with Chaz?"

"No," Cisco said. "He's fine."

"So, where is he?" Melody asked eagerly, jumping up from the bench, her exhaustion completely gone. "I hope that I can see him before I get beamed back Down Below."

Cisco made a vague gesture with her hand. "Dang, it'll be near impossible to find him in this huge place," she drawled, her Tennessee accent getting thicker.

"Cisco—" Melody began.

"What?"

"Your accent," Melody said. "When you're really, really mad and when you're lying are the two times your accent gets really thick."

"I've noticed that, too," Nicole agreed.

Cisco nudged Nicole hard in the ribs.

"Oh, now you guys really have me worried," Melody said, clutching her hands together. "What's going on?"

"Nothing!" Cisco exclaimed. "I'm just saying he'd be really hard to find. You'll see him on your next—"

"Are you kidding?" Melody replied. "I'm going to find him now. Is there someplace we can all meet later?"

Again, Melody saw Nicole and Cisco exchange a quick glance.

"You did it again!" Melody exclaimed. "That look!"

"What look?" Cisco asked.

Melody folded her arms. "Cisco McCaine, you are a Teen Angel. And Teen Angels don't lie."

"Oh, please," Cisco snorted. "I'm no more angelic now than I was on Earth, and you know it."

"Well, I'm going to find Chaz," Melody insisted. "Where can we meet up?"

"There's, uh, a food court in the center of all this," Cisco replied. "You just follow the golden arches painted on the walkway."

"Great!" Melody said. "We'll meet there at eleven o'clock. If I'm still here, that is."

"Great," Cisco and Nicole responded, at the same time, though their tone of voice was very very strange.

"So I'm going to go find Chaz now," Melody told her friends. "See you later, OK?"

"Oh, no—" Nicole muttered under her breath, looking past Melody at something. Her normally pale complexion grew even paler.

Melody turned around to see what had upset Nicole.

And there, just getting into line for the huge roller coaster was Chaz Denton.

And with him was none other than Scarlett Whitmore.

"I think I feel sick," Melody whispered, her hands over her stomach.

"Look, it doesn't mean anything—" Cisco began.

"I have eyes," Melody said. "They're together, aren't they? This is why you guys were acting so strange."

"But it really doesn't mean anything," Nicole insisted.

"She's so horrid," Melody said, a catch in her voice. "I just don't understand. Do you?"

"She hasn't been horrid," Nicole said in a small voice.

"Ha!" Melody exclaimed. "I know Scarlett. Scarlett is horrid. I'm sorry if that isn't an angelic thing to say, but it's the truth."

Melody watched as Scarlett laughed at something Chaz said, putting her head on his shoulder for a moment.

"Maybe dying changed her or something," Nicole said. "Because she's been . . . nice."

"Scarlett?" Melody breathed. "Nice?"

Cisco and Nicole nodded.

"I keep waiting for her to turn into this witch," Cisco said, "and it just doesn't happen."

Tears came to Melody's eyes. "You mean to tell me that Scarlett has managed to get my boyfriend and my two best friends, too?"

"Oh, Mel, it isn't like that—" Nicole began.

But Melody wasn't listening. *For once in my life I'm going to be assertive*, she vowed. And then she turned on her heel and marched right over to Chaz and Scarlett.

"Melody!" Chaz exclaimed when he saw her. He hugged her quickly, but she remained stiff in his arms.

"It looks as if you two are having fun," Melody said in a cold voice.

"Oh, we are!" Scarlett assured her, as if everything was perfectly normal.

"Did you finish your mission?" Chaz asked.

"No," Melody said. "I'm here temporarily and I have no idea why. Imagine the coincidence of running into the two of you. Together."

Scarlett looked at Chaz and smiled. "It was so nice of Chaz to agree to walk around with me," she said in a soft sweet voice. "I know how much he'd rather have been with you."

"This place is so cool, Mel!" Chaz enthused. "We've got to come here together sometime!"

"We're here together right now," Melody said, her voice stony.

"Oh, gee, I should let the two of you be alone," Scarlett said. "Who knows when JD will beam you back Down Below."

"Are you sure you don't mind?" Chaz asked.

"Not at all!" Scarlett insisted. "I'll go find my roommate, Celeste. I think she's kind of lonely, so it'll be a good thing to do. Nice to see you, Melody! Good luck on your mission!" Scarlett hurried away from them.

Melody's jaw dropped open. "Are you sure that was Scarlett Whitmore?"

"It's incredible, isn't it?" Chaz asked. "I think dying did her a world of good! She's really, really nice!"

"I don't believe it," Melody said, folding her arms.

"But it's true!" Chaz insisted. "Everyone says so."

"It has to be an act," Melody decided.

"Oh, come on, Mel, that isn't worthy of you," Chaz chided her. "You believe people can change for the better, don't you?"

"I guess so," Melody said grudgingly. "I just

don't know if Scarlett Whitmore can change for the better."

Chaz put his arms around Melody's waist, and gently pulled her to him. "You don't have to worry about Scarlett. She's just a friend."

"How close a friend?" Melody asked.

"Not as close as this," Chaz said. And he bent over and gave her a soft, sexy kiss.

"Oh, Chaz, I—"

Next in line, please get into the next car," the mechanical voice intoned. Melody realized with a start that they were still in line for the roller coaster.

"Want to?" Chaz asked.

"Not a chance!" Melody said, pulling Chaz out of the line.

"I already rode it three times with Scarlett," Chaz said. "It was fun!"

"With Scarlett?" Melody echoed, something terrible burning in her stomach.

"Mel, come on," Chaz said. "You can't really believe you have anything to be jealous about!"

"I'm not jealous," Melody said, her cheeks burning with heat.

"Good," Chaz said. "Because Scarlett really has changed. And I think we have to be big enough not to hold her past against her."

"Right," Melody agreed, even though she still felt as if she had swallowed a pitcherful of acid and it was churning around in her stomach.

"Good," Chaz said, hugging Melody. "I knew you could do it."

Melody hugged Chaz back, but inside she felt terrible, guilty, angry, and scared.

I don't believe Scarlett has changed, she thought. *And I do hold her past against her.*

Now, what kind of a terrible Teen Angel does that make me?

Seven

"Melody, are you okay?" Emily asked, staring up at Melody, her eyes wide with fear.

"Huh?"

"You got this really funny look on your face," Emily explained. "And then you kind of screamed, and then you wouldn't move."

Melody blinked and shook her head quickly. She looked around. There she was, back once again at the Happy Days Daycare Center.

But why was I beamed to TeenHeavenWorld? Melody wondered. *JD didn't even show up at the amusement park, so what was the point? One minute I was telling a huge lie, that I agreed with Chaz that Scarlett had changed, and the next instant I'm back here again.*

This is enough to make me crazy.

"Do you want me to get Mrs. Plant?" Emily asked with concern.

"No, no, I'm fine," Melody assured the little girl, even though she didn't know if that was entirely true. "So, you were going to lead me to the snacks, weren't you?"

"Sure," said Emily. "I just hope Duane didn't eat them all already." She motioned for Melody to lean down so she could whisper in her ear. "He steals food. And then he barfs it all up later."

"Yuck," Melody said, straightening up. She was at a loss for words.

"I know just what you mean," Emily agreed solemnly.

Melody smiled because the little girl was so cute, but her mind was still back at Teen-HeavenWorld with Chaz.

Chaz. Who now thought that Scarlett Whitmore was the nicest girl in Teen Heaven.

At six o'clock, when Melody slowly climbed the front porch steps of the Red Lion Inn, every bone in her body hurt. Her head was pounding. Her feet were screaming. And her formerly white jeans were now so filthy that she doubted they'd ever be clean again. True to Emily's prediction, The Doody-Bomb Kid had hurled midafternoon, just as Melody was about to wash his hands at the sink in the corner of the room. It happened without warning. And it happened all over Melody.

She'd tried her best to get it all off of her, but telltale stains still remained.

"Wow, you look terrible," Meredith said, as Melody plopped her body down in the nearest empty wicker rocking chair.

"I feel even worse than that," Melody replied. "Who ever thought that taking care of a bunch of kids could be so tough?"

"It's the toughest," Meredith agreed, balancing her tray on her hip. "I plan to have only one child, and I also plan to be really, really rich so that I can have full-time help."

"What kind of career are you planning where you'll make that kind of money?" Melody asked, closing her eyes with exhaustion.

"Social worker," Meredith admitted.

Melody opened her eyes and looked at her, and they both laughed.

"I know," Meredith said. "Social workers don't make any money. Oh well, so I'm living in a dream world! You want a cold drink or something?"

"Ice tea would be heavenly," Melody said gratefully.

"Be right back," Meredith replied, and hurried back into the Inn.

Melody closed her eyes again, her mind drifting, until she felt a tap on her shoulder.

"I don't mean to bother you..."

Melody looked over at a middle-aged man in the next rocking chair, slender, with white hair and a small, white goatee. "Yes?" she said politely.

"I couldn't help overhearing that you're in room twenty," the man said, his deep-set eyes boring into Melody's.

"When did you hear that?" Melody asked carefully.

"Last night," the man said. "I was sitting on that couch behind you when you were talking with that young waitess, and I overheard you. I hope you don't find this too intrusive."

"No, it's all right," Melody said, although she wasn't really sure.

I really do have to learn to stand up for myself and not worry so much about what people will think of me, she thought quickly.

"But why were you listening in on our conversation?" she forced herself to add.

"I do apologize," the man said. "I should introduce myself. I'm Dr. Albert Frazier, and I'm a parapsychologist."

"What's that?" Melody asked.

"A scholar who studies paranormal phenomenon," he explained.

"I still don't know what you're talking about," Melody admitted.

"Ghosts, among other things," Dr. Frazier said. "I had heard about the hauntings in room twenty from my sister—she's lived in Stockbridge for twenty years, and I was hoping to study the room."

"Couldn't you just rent it, then?" Melody asked politely.

"I have," Dr. Frazier said. "But ghosts are very smart. They know I'm there to find them out, and so whenever I stay in the room, they don't show up."

"Maybe there just aren't any ghosts in there," Melody said.

"Oh, there are," Dr. Frazier insisted. "I could feel their vibrations." He leaned closer to her. "Did you notice anything unusual in your room last night?"

"Not a thing," Melody said.

"No strange scents, no blasts of cold air without the window being opened? No cackling laughter—"

"Wait, there was... some laughter," Melody admitted.

"Aha!" Dr. Frazier exclaimed. "That's one of their tricks!"

"Oh, no, I think it was just someone in the hallway—" Melody protested.

"Did it sound as if it came from the hallway?" Dr. Frazier demanded.

"Well, no, not really," Melody said. "But I don't think—"

"It came from the closet, right?" Dr. Frazier asked.

A chill swept over Melody. "How did you know that?"

"I picked up the vibrations," Dr. Frazier said. "The ghost is in the closet. I'm sure of it."

"You are?" Melody asked, alarmed.

"Positive," Dr. Frazier said. "You must try to get the ghost to show himself to you tonight!"

"But... what can... can ghosts do to you?" Melody asked, scared in spite of herself.

"It depends," Dr. Franzer said gravely.

"On what?"

"On how malevolent the ghost is," Dr. Frazier said.

"Ma—what?" Melody asked.

"Evil," Dr. Frazier said. "How evil."

"Here's your iced tea," Meredith said cheerfully, handing Melody her drink. "Oh, hi, Dr. Frazier," she added.

"Meredith, do you realize this child is staying in room twenty all by herself?" Dr. Frazier demanded.

"Oh, it's fine," Meredith assured Dr. Frazier.

"Melody doesn't even believe in ghosts. Do you, Melody?"

"No," Melody said, though she could hear her voice shaking a little. "I don't."

"See?" Meredith said. "Excuse me, I've got customers." She hurried off.

"But you should believe," Dr. Frazier insisted, leaning even closer to Melody. "Because they hurt those who don't believe."

"Oh, come on . . ." Melody began.

"There are some very, very bad ghosts," Dr. Frazier continued. "They belong in another world, an evil world, but somehow they got stuck halfway between that world and this one . . ."

Does he mean Deep Six? Melody wondered anxiously. *Is it possible that a ghost who belongs in Deep Six could be haunting room twenty? No, that's silly. I'm letting myself get carried away because I'm so exhausted . . .*

"I'm telling you the truth!" Dr. Frazier continued, reaching out to clutch Melody's arm. "I have spent a lifetime studying these things! There is an evil, evil ghost haunting room twenty. A ghost that could do terrible things to you! You have to believe me!"

Melody jumped up, eager to get away from Dr. Frazier's strange intensity. "Please excuse me," she said in her breathy, little girl voice. "I mean, it was very nice to have met you, but I need to go—"

"Is that rocking chair taken?" a throaty female voice asked.

Melody looked up.

And what she saw almost made her faint.

Because she was staring into the cold, flat eyes of Payton Fire.

Payton Fire. From Deep Six. The girl the Bad Dude had sent up to Ground Zero to try and thwart Cisco's first mission.

But Melody knew Payton wasn't really a girl. She was a changling, meaning she could be sent to Earth in any shape or form that the Bad Dude chose.

Although Payton would appear normal to humans, Teen Angels could see that like everyone from Deep Six, she had no pupils to her eyes.

"You!" Melody gasped.

Payton smiled a cold, evil smile. She was beautiful, her long brown hair flowing down her back, her cat's eyes burning brightly.

But Melody knew how truly ugly Payton Fire really was.

"Have we met?" Payton asked innocently. "I just wanted to know if your rocking chair was free."

Melody whirled around to Dr. Frazier. "What do you see when you look at her?" she demanded.

"A very attractive young woman," Dr. Frazier said, looking confused.

"Why, thank you," Payton said, slipping past Melody to sit in the rocking chair she had vacated.

Melody turned and backed away, her eyes on Payton.

"Nice to have met you, whoever you are," Payton called to Melody. "Oh, one other thing."

"What?" Melody asked, her voice coming out as a whisper of fear.

"Good luck in room twenty tonight," Payton said, an evil smile playing across her lips. "You'll need it."

"JD!" Melody called, for maybe the hundredth time. "Please! How am I supposed to go to sleep with Payton Fire after me?"

She stared up at the ceiling of the infamous room twenty, willing JD to show up and tell her what to do.

But once again only the silence greeted her.

"But I'm scared," Melody admitted in a little voice, reaching for her pillow. She squeezed it tightly to her chest. "I wish Chaz was here. No, not Chaz. He's probably busy telling Scarlett Whitmore a good-night story. Cisco, that's who I need. She's the bravest person I know." She looked up at the ceiling again. "JD, couldn't you please send Cisco down to help me? Please?"

Nothing.

Melody sighed and slowly crawled under the covers. She had changed into some flannel pajamas, and even though she was totally exhausted, she felt as if every nerve in her body was standing at attention.

Okay, you've got to get ahold of yourself, she thought. *You are a Teen Angel. That means the Big Guy is looking out for you. You are not alone. You have to believe that the Big Guy is more powerful than the Bad Dude, and He's not going to let anything bad happen to you.*

Melody forced herself to lie down in the bed, her eyes staring up at the ceiling. Then, her arm rigid, she reached over and turned off the light near the bed.

Bizarre shadows danced across the ceiling.

Relax, she told herself. *It's just shadows from the trees outside. Relax and go to sleep. You have another tough day at the daycare center tomorrow.*

Melody took a deep breath, and one by one willed her muscles to unclench and relax. She could feel her breath growing deeper, and finally her mind began to drift, until she was in a relaxed half-asleep-half-awake state.

"Ohhhhhhhhhhhh!"

Melody bolted upright in bed.

She had just heard a long, terrible groan, so agonized that it could only come from a creature in terrible, excruciating pain.

And it had come right from the closet.

Eight

"Who's in there?" Melody yelled, clutching her pillow with white-knuckled fingers.

Silence.

"JD," Melody whispered, her teeth practically clanging against each other. "JD, you have to come help me!"

More silence.

Melody felt as if she was listening with every fiber of her body. *Maybe I imagined it*, she told herself. *It's perfectly silent now, so maybe the whole thing was just my imagination playing tr—*

"OO-oo-oo-oo-oo!" a long, plaintive moan came from the closet.

Melody screamed and jumped out of bed, still clutching her pillow. In a flash she was across the room and out the door of her room, standing in the hall in nothing but her flannel pajamas, still clutching her pillow. Her breath came in shallow gasps. Her hands shook.

"Are you okay, miss?" A middle-aged man stood in the hallway, about to go into a room two doors down.

Suddenly Melody realized she was hardly dressed and clutching a pillow like an idiot.

What am I supposed to tell him, that a ghost drove me out of my room? she thought miserably. "I'm fine," she managed, trying for a smile and failing.

"Are you sure?" he asked, cocking his head at her. "You're white as a ghost!"

The man smiled and took a few steps towards Melody, and then a terrible thought hit her.

What if he's from Deep Six? What if he's coming over here to do something terrible to me?

The man stepped closer, and shadows from the ancient chandelier that hung from the ceiling cast crazy shadows on his face.

"Maybe I can help—" the man said in a low voice.

"No!" Melody yelled, sure now that he was from Deep Six, not waiting for him to get close enough to do the eyeball test. She ran back into her room and bolted the door, standing against it, breathing hard.

Melody eyed the closet where she had heard the terrible moaning. Then she thought about what awaited her in the hallway.

Which was worse?

"JD, please!" Melody called plaintively. "I know I'm not the galaxy's best Teen Angel, but I'm trying! Are you punishing me for Scarlett Whitmore? Because I really am trying to be nice to her now, and—"

"These middle-of-the-night monologues have got to go, babe," JD said.

Melody looked around. No JD. Only his voice.

"JD!" Melody cried with relief. "Where are you?"

"Try the TV," JD suggested.

Melody looked over at the cabinet that housed the TV. Nothing. "I don't see you."

"I mean *on* the TV," JD explained. "Literally."

Melody took a few steps to the center of her room where she could see the TV screen that had been blocked by the door of the cabinet. And sure enough, the TV was now on, and JD's face smiled back at her.

"Wow," Melody breathed. "That's so amazing."

"Frankly, I didn't have the energy to zap myself to your room right at the moment," JD admitted. "What a day I had! I was in a meeting with the Big Guy, and I get word that this Teen Angel on a mission is getting seriously jerked around by some Deep Sixers. So the Big Guy tells me to go take care of it, which I do, and then—"

"JD, I'm sorry you had a bad day," Melody interrupted, "but I'm the one who needs help now!"

JD beamed at her. "See? I knew you could be assertive if you put your mind to it."

Melody sighed. "You're constantly testing us, aren't you?"

"Hey, it's not me, babe. It's much bigger than that, if you catch my drift. So anyway, what's with all the plaintive wailing?"

"I saw Payton Fire from Deep Six!" Melody cried. "And then I met this man who told me this room is haunted by an evil ghost, and then I heard these terrible sounds coming from the closet, and then there was this man in the hallway and I thought he might be a Deep Sixer, and then—"

"Hold up, hold up," JD interrupted. "One scary thing at a time, okay?"

Melody took a deep breath. "This room is haunted," she told JD.

"Oh, yeah?" JD asked. "Cool! Did you meet the ghost yet?"

"This is not funny, JD!" Melody insisted. "Hey, wait a second. Are you telling me that there really *are* ghosts?"

"Whatever," JD said with a shrug.

"What kind of answer is that?" Melody yelled. "It's the middle of the night and I'm really tired, and I'm scared, and ... and ... you're not helping!"

JD smiled again. "Wow, this assertive thing is really taking hold, babe! I'm proud of you!"

Melody sighed and sat wearily on the bed. "JD, please. What am I supposed to do?"

"Your mission," JD said.

"But ... am I in danger?" Melody asked. "I was so scared ..."

"Well, I'm not gonna lie to you about Payton Fire," JD said. "When she's around, any Teen Angel has to watch her back. But that doesn't mean you can't handle it."

"Yes, it does!" Melody insisted. "I'm no match for the Bad Dude!"

"This is where faith comes in real handy," JD pointed out. "And you're more of a match for His Badness than you realize."

"Oh, I'm not, JD," Melody said sadly. "I don't have any powers. Most of the time I don't even feel as if I deserve to be a Teen Angel at all." She looked down at her hands in her lap. "How's everything up there?" she asked carefully.

"Everything's cool," JD said casually. "But then you know that, you were just at TeenHeavenWorld."

"Right," Melody agreed. "It was fun."

JD nodded. "Scarlett's really starting to fit in, too. Isn't that great?"

"Oh, sure," Melody said, trying to sound as if she meant it. "That's great. I guess she's changing into a nicer person. That's what Chaz says."

"Well, he should know, he hangs out with her a lot," JD said.

But why? Melody wanted to scream. *Why are you doing this to me all over again, JD? It was bad enough that Chaz had to pretend to be her boyfriend Down Below, but why is this happening in Teen Heaven? Can't you stop it? Can't you do something?*

Or maybe you're not doing it to me. It's just Chaz. Chaz and Scarlett. They like each other now. She's changed. And she's so pretty. And she's up there and I'm down here and—

There was so much Melody wanted to say, but she knew she couldn't say a word. Not and be any kind of a Teen Angel at all.

"So, you feel better now that I made my brief but miraculous appearance?" JD asked Melody.

"A little," Melody said. "But I still want to know what's in the closet."

"Your clothes," JD smirked.

"Besides that," Melody said.

"Here's what you need to get," JD explained. "The Big Guy is watching over you. We're not talking a wimp power here, know what I mean?

You think the Big Guy is going to let you down?"

"I'm more worried about letting the Big Guy down," Melody admitted. "I know I should be brave, but . . . I'm not."

"Mel, Mel, Mel," JD chided her gently. "You don't give yourself enough credit. Cut yourself some slack, huh?"

"I'll try," Melody said softly.

"Cool," JD replied. "So, I'm off like a dirty shirt. You're doing real good down there, Mel. Hang in, okay?"

"Yes, but is the guy in the hallway from—"

The TV was blank, black, and turned off.

Melody sighed again. "Great," she murmured. "Just great. He didn't give me any answers about anything."

She eyed the closet warily, then mustered up all her courage. *I am a Teen Angel*, she told herself. *The Big Guy is looking after me. I'm not afraid of noises in a closet. And now I'm going back to sleep.*

And even though she was sure her assertions were pure bravado, that she'd never even be able to even close her eyes, Melody quickly found herself falling into a deep and dreamless sleep.

"Melody, Henry wee-weed in the sandbox!"

"Melody, I can't find my pink Play-Doh. I think Heather ate it!"

"Melody, play with me, okay?"

"No, me!"

"Me, me, meeee!"

"I asked first, you doody-bomb!"

"At Happy Days we all are friends! . . ."

It was the next afternoon. Melody put her

hand to her forehead, which was throbbing, just as it had the day before. *Who ever knew that taking care of little kids was such tough work?* she thought, glancing over at the clock.

"Want me to get you a glass of juice?" little Emily asked Melody, reaching shyly for her hand.

Melody smiled at the little girl. "It's not snack time yet."

"I know," Emily replied solemnly. "But whenever my mommy puts her hand up to her forehead like that it means she has a bad headache, and then she likes for me to get her juice."

Melody crouched down and gave Emily a quick hug. "You're terrific, Emily, know that?"

"Hug me!" a little girl wailed, and tried to force her way between Melody and Emily.

"No, me!" another girl yelled.

"Me, me, me!" the Doody-Bomb Kid insisted.

Melody laughed. Suddenly her headache was gone. "I have an idea," she told them, straightening up. "Why don't we do a group hug? That way everyone can get hugged at the same time!"

"Yeahhhhhh!" the little kids cried.

"Okay, everyone put your arms out," Melody instructed them. "Now we'll all smush up together and on the count of three, we'll have the world's biggest hug!"

"Yeahhhhhh!" they all yelled again.

"Here goes," Melody said. "One, two, three . . . hug!"

Squealing with laughter and happiness, the little kids all hugged each other.

"Well, I feel much better," Melody told them. "How about you guys?"

"Henry still wee-weed in the sandbox!" Heather explained with exasperation, her hands on her tiny hips.

The rest of the day passed quickly, as the kids got more used to being with Melody. They went outside and found beautiful leaves, which they glued into a book. They did fingerpainting, which was messy but incredibly fun, and they acted out animals from a story book. All in all it was an exhausting but satisfying day.

"Melody, can you wait in the playground with the little ones for their parents to pick them up?" Mrs. Plant asked, as she helped a little girl into her sweater.

"Sure," Melody agreed.

"Meredith is coming for me today," Emily said, putting her hand in Melody's as they walked out to the playground. "Mommy is at work."

"It'll be nice to see her," Melody said.

"She's so pretty," Emily said. "And she's smart, too. She gets all As in school."

"That's great," Melody said, sitting down on a swing.

"Did you get As in school?" Emily asked, sitting on the next swing.

"I wasn't a very good student," Melody admitted. "I wish I had been."

"Didn't you study?" Emily asked, wide-eyed.

"Not as much as I should have," Melody said. *How can I explain that I was always off doing some modeling job?* she thought to herself. *It would probably sound wonderful and glamorous to a little girl, when it really wasn't anything like that at all . . .*

"'Bye, you guys!" Henry yelled cheerfully, as he walked off with his mother.

More and more parents arrived, until only little Emily was left on the playground.

"You're sure Meredith was supposed to get you?" Melody asked, glancing at her watch. Meredith was about thirty minutes late. Since the daycare imposed a financial penalty if parents were late to pick up the kids, they were usually picked up very promptly.

"Yep, that's what Mommy told me at breakfast," Emily said in a small voice. "Do you think she forgot?"

"Oh, no, I'm sure she didn't," Melody said. "Anyway, don't worry. I promise to stay with you until she comes, no matter what."

"Thanks," Emily said, cuddling up to Melody.

Mrs. Plant came out of the building, locking the door behind her. She glanced around and saw that Melody and Emily were still in the playground.

"Oh, I thought everyone was gone," she said, walking over to Melody and Emily.

"I'll wait with Emily, it's fine," Melody assured her.

Mrs. Plant looked at her watch. "Oh, dear, I have a dental appointment..."

"It really is okay," Melody assured her. "And I have a key Tarshea gave me to the daycare, in case we need to go inside and use the phone or anything."

"Well, if you're certain..." Mrs. Plant began.

"It's fine," Melody said.

"All right, then. I'll see you tomorrow." Mrs.

Plant walked off to her car in the rear parking lot.

"So, Emily," Melody began, wanting to distract the little girl from worrying about why her sister was late, "what do you want to be when you grow up?"

"A doctor who takes care of sick people," Emily said promptly, swinging a little in her swing.

"That's a wonderful idea!" Melody said.

Emily nodded. "You give them shots and tell them what pills to take and then they get better."

"Right," Melody agreed. She pushed her feet into the dirt below her and let herself swing back and forth.

"What do you want to be when you grow up?" Emily asked her.

I'm never going to grow up, she thought. *Not anymore.*

But, of course, she couldn't say that.

"Oh, I don't know," Melody said lightly. "I guess my plans aren't as definite as yours are."

"Hi, there," a cute young guy said, ambling over to them. He looked to be about eighteen, and he had brown hair that fell over his forehead. He wore hip-looking wraparound sunglasses.

"Hello," Emily said politely. "Who are you?"

"Kevin Cravens," he said. "Oh, come on, Emily, you must remember me. I'm a friend of your big sister Meredith's!"

Emily stared up at him. "I don't think I remember you."

"Well, you just broke my heart," he said easily. He smiled at Melody. "Hi, you must be Melody, right?"

She nodded.

"Meredith told me all about you. You're staying at the Red Lion Inn, right?"

Melody nodded again.

"Meredith got tied up at work. She called me and asked me to come pick up Emily. Hey, what are friends for, you know?"

"But . . . I'm only authorized to release Emily to a family member," Melody said slowly.

"Listen, I totally understand," Kevin agreed. "You can't be too careful when it comes to kids. That's why I brought a note that Meredith wrote, so you'd know this is cool."

Kevin handed Melody a piece of stationery from the Red Lion Inn that basically said Kevin was picking Emily up from daycare, and it was signed by Meredith.

"Is this your sister's handwriting?" Melody asked, showing the note to Emily.

Emily shrugged and eyed Kevin warily.

"I'm sorry," Melody said, handing him back the note, "but I can't release her to you. I mean, she says she doesn't even know you!"

Kevin sighed. "How about if you call Meredith at the Red Lion?" he suggested. He reached into his back pocket and took out a very small, compact cellular phone, then he quickly gave Melody the phone number.

The line was busy.

"Look, even if she told me over the phone that you are who you say you are," Melody said, handing Kevin back his phone, "I'm sorry, but I still wouldn't feel right about this. She'd have to tell me herself, in person."

Kevin shook his head. "She's gonna be pretty ticked off about this."

Emily crept off her swing and edged over toward Melody, putting her little hand in Melody's hand.

"I'm sorry," Melody said again, holding Emily's hand fast.

"Whoa, look at that!" Kevin cried, pointing behind them.

Melody turned to look, and just at that moment she felt Emily's hand ripped from hers.

"No!" Emily yelled.

Melody turned back quickly, to see that Kevin had grabbed the little girl and torn her from Melody's grasp.

And in doing so, his sunglasses had fallen to the ground, and Melody was staring into his eyes.

The eyes of evil. The eyes of no pupils. The eyes of Deep Six.

Nine

Melody was frozen in place as surely as if her two feet were bolted to the ground.

She was a human ice sculpture.

It was like some invisible force was absolutely gluing her to where she stood. Even though she knew that if she was going to have any hope of saving Emily from the horrible creature from Deep Six she would have to act quickly, she couldn't move at all.

Emily screamed.

"HEEEELLLLP!" she cried, as Kevin turned, viciously pulling the little girl behind him.

"Shaddup!" Kevin yelled at her, trying to increase his speed. "Just shaddup!" His voice was harsh and gutteral.

"HEELLLLP!" the little girl screamed again, snapping her head back toward Melody, tears streaming down her face. "MELODY, HEEELP ME!"

Her plaintive cry echoed off some nearby buildings. But then Kevin's cackling laughter swallowed up the sounds of the little girl's fear.

He pulled at her harshly, dragging the screaming girl along with him.

"No, no, no!" Emily yelled, sobs caught in her throat.

Oh, please, please, I have to help her, Melody thought, pain and fear coursing through her body. *Why can't I move? Why?*

"Let go!" Emily shrieked, and she yanked hard on Kevin's hand. For just a moment she almost got free, as Kevin lost his balance and stumbled over a broken brick.

But instantly he righted himself, and grabbed Emily by her arm, clutching hard.

"Melody! Melody, help me!" Emily cried again.

Each word was like a knife in Melody's heart. And still, she couldn't move.

"Yeah, Mel-Oh-Dee," Kevin called back, his voice even more gutteral and terrifying now. "Why don't you help her? Why don't you get some heavenly help? Ha-ha-ha-ha-ha! Mel-Oh-Dee."

It was the most evil laughter that Melody had ever heard.

I've got to do something, but I can't move, Melody thought, dumbstruck. *I want to more than anything, but I can't move! Please, oh please, JD, if ever you were going to help me, help me now!*

Melody opened her mouth to try and call to Emily, but, as if she were in some horrible nightmare, no sound came from Melody's throat.

I can't even talk. I can't even open my mouth to say anything.

Emily dug her heels into the dirt, as Kevin continued to drag her toward the street. And now,

Melody watched, still frozen, as Kevin yanked the four-year-old's left arm so hard that the girl yelled in pain and shock.

"Melody, you have to do something. You have the power."

Huh? Who's that? Melody thought, wondering who had spoken to her, turning around behind her towards the sound of the voice.

Nothing.

There was no one there.

But suddenly, Melody realized that she had turned her head to listen for the voice. Which meant that she could move again.

Who was that?

I have to do something, Melody thought, quickly and automatically now bolting after Kevin and Emily. *I have to get to her. I have to, I have to!*

Melody ran as fast as she could, but Kevin continued to run, pulling Emily behind him. Emily kept yelling, and her yells were now mixed with sobs. She fought against Kevin as hard as she could, which impeded his progress across the uneven terrain of the schoolyard.

"Help me, Melody!" she pleaded, "help me!"

"I'm coming!" Melody cried back, running after her, quickly kicking the clogs off her feet as she ran so they wouldn't slow her down. "I'm coming!"

Melody heard Kevin curse as she ran as fast as she could toward the evil changling and the little girl.

But even as she ran, the doubts kept piling up in her mind, even as she got closer and closer to the guy from Deep Six and the little girl she had come to love so much.

I'm not an athlete, how can I be running after them?

He's so much bigger than me, he's going to hurt me when I get there.

How was I frozen in place? Can he do it again to me?

I can never save her. Never.

Can't JD or Cisco or Chaz, or somebody like the Big Guy, help me now? No, don't help me. Help Emily. Please?

"I'm coming," Melody repeated, gasping for air now as she ran, feeling a terrible cramp developing in her right side.

"Yeah, right!" Kevin called back. He turned his head toward Melody, and now he looked nothing like the cute guy who had tried to pass himself off as a friend of Meredith's. Horns sprouted from the top of his head, his eyeballs leaked blood and pus, and rivulets of pea-green slime ran from the gaping wound that his mouth had become.

"I'm warning you," Kevin called, in a voice that now sounded as if it had been ripped from the pits of hell, "don't get any closer, Angel!"

Ignore him, Melody told herself. *He's trying to scare you. Don't look into his eyes.* A wave of revulsion passed through her. *Do anything, but don't look in his eyes!*

Melody kept running after them, feeling arrows of pain shoot up her legs as her feet came crashing down on all sorts of stones and rocks.

But she was gaining on them. Since Emily kept twisting and turning away from Kevin, he couldn't move all that quickly.

And now it looked as if Melody might actually have a chance.

Please, JD, Melody thought, as she marshaled every bit of power and strength that was inside her, *please* . . .

And then, with an incredible burst of speed, she was right behind Kevin and Emily.

"Melody! Help me!" Emily cried, now exhausted, out of breath, and absolutely petrified with fear. She reached one hand out toward Melody. It was clear the little girl couldn't fight much longer.

I only have one chance, Melody thought. *Only one.* And then, without allowing herself to consider the possibly horrible consequences should she fail, Melody dove to make a tackle, just like she'd seen so many football players do on television games that she'd watched while she was alive, usually sitting next to some guy she didn't like who was paying much more attention to some stupid game on television than he was paying to Melody, the girl sitting next to him.

She dove.

And she tackled Emily, whom Kevin still held onto by the arm.

It happened so quickly that Kevin was caught by surprise, and as Melody and the little girl went crashing to the ground, Emily's hand was torn from Kevin's grasp.

Kevin cursed. Loudly and profusely.

"You damned Angel," Kevin growled. His voice was angry, but he now looked like the same, normal guy who had shown up and tried to get Emily to leave with him.

"He can't get you now," Melody said, rocking

the little girl in her arms. "He can't get you."

Suddenly, a weirdly beatific look came over Kevin's face. Even though he'd been running just as hard and just as long as Melody, and even though he had been breathing heavily too, his breath became measured. Easy. Even tranquil.

He walked back to them and smiled down at them on the ground. "This isn't over yet," he said, his smile turning into a broad grin. "Later." Then, he turned to the left, walking quickly, until he disappeared around a corner.

I can't believe it, Melody thought, in absolute wonder. *He was from Deep Six, he came after Emily and me, and—*

"He tried to hurt me, Melody!" Emily cried, snuggling fearfully into Melody's arms. "Why was he trying to hurt me?"

"It's okay," Melody crooned to the girl, her voice soothing and comforting. "It's okay."

"But he hurted me," Emily managed to say, in between her sobs.

"I know," Melody said to her, putting her arms even tighter around the little girl and rocking her, even as the two of them lay together on a grassy meridian strip between the sidewalk and the street. "I know. He was a bad person. A very bad person."

"What happened?" Meredith cried, running over to them. She took in the sight of her sobbing, little sister and Melody on the ground. "Oh my God, what happened?"

"Everything is okay now," Melody assured her, since Meredith looked about ready to faint.

Meredith fell to her knees, and wrapped her arms around the two of them. "But what happened? I am so sorry I'm late," she said, over and over. "I am so, so sorry."

"Not as sorry as I am," Melody said quietly. And then, she took one arm, put it around Emily, and one around Meredith, and it was like the group hug that she'd done with the kids in the daycare center, earlier.

Only it was a whole, whole lot more important.

"We have to go to the police," Meredith said firmly. "Now. Right away."

It won't do any good, Melody thought. *What am I going to say to them? Oh, it was a changeling from Deep Six, but I am sure that if I give you his description, you'll catch him, and if you don't, just ask JD for some help?*

It was ten minutes later. Meredith, Emily, and Melody sat together on the front stoop of Happy Days Daycare Center. Both Meredith and Melody had an arm around little Emily. The good news was that the little girl seemed to be regaining her composure very quickly.

Melody had, in the most detail that she could recall, recounted to Meredith the story of what had happened, leaving out the part about how she felt she'd been frozen in place by some supernatural force, and how she'd heard some voice telling her that she had to do something to save the little girl.

"We've got to go to the police," Meredith repeated. "Right away."

"He said Melody was an angel," Emily told her sister, holding tightly to her sister's hand.

Meredith laughed. "Maybe she is," Meredith

chuckled. "Maybe she's your angel."

"If I was an angel," Melody said nonchalantly, "I'm the world's dumbest angel. I should have flown away with your sister. And not gotten all bruised up." She looked ruefully down at her feet, which were bloodied by the rocks she'd stepped on, and at her legs, which were dirty and bruised from where she'd landed on her flying tackle of the little girl.

"Why didn't anyone come when I screamed?" Emily asked in a small voice.

"Maybe no one heard you, honey," Meredith said soothingly.

"But I screamed really, really loud, didn't I, Melody?" Emily asked.

"You did," Melody agreed.

"So I don't know why people didn't come help me," Emily said, her bottom lip quivering.

Melody shook her head. *How do I explain to a little child that people just want to stay away from trouble?* she thought. *How do I tell her that people on Earth are so afraid that sometimes even when a little child is crying for help, it falls on deaf ears?*

"We're going to the police," Meredith announced. "Now." She got up purposefully.

"But are you sure—" Melody began.

"Of course I'm sure!" Meredith said. "That maniac is still out there! I just need to call the Inn and tell them I'll be late." She reached down to hug her little sister. "Don't worry, Emily. We're going to catch whoever tried to steal you. We won't let him get away with it."

Melody didn't say a word. She just sent up a prayer that there really was something they could do to stop him.

Ten

"I gotta hand it to you, babe, I am seriously impressed," JD told Melody. He was leaning against a dresser, popping Milk Duds in his mouth from a large box. "Milk Dud?" he offered.

Melody stood before him, utterly discombobulated and confused. "Wait. Am I awake or am I dreaming?" Melody asked. A cramp hit her left leg, and she bent over to rub it gingerly, careful to keep her fingers off the cuts and bruises she'd acquired during her ordeal with Kevin the changeling.

"Awake," JD confirmed, as he popped another Milk Dud into his mouth. "And back up on your favorite cloud." He looked deep into his box of candy. "Man, I can't believe I ate this whole box. Gotta do something about those sugar cravings." He threw the box over his shoulder and it made a perfect landing in the wastepaper basket.

"I have a terrible cramp," Melody said, still rubbing her leg.

"Hmmm, maybe I zapped you too fast," JD said. He snapped his fingers and a tube of BEN-

GAY appeared in his hands, which he then handed over to Melody.

She rubbed some into her calf and looked around the room, trying to reorient herself.

I'm back here, in my room in Teen Heaven, she thought, looking around the familiar space. *JD zapped me back here. I was—*

"So, what do you remember?" JD asked, pulling a pack of sugarless gum out of his back pocket.

What do I remember? I went to the Stockbridge police with Emily and Meredith, and we told them everything. We even gave them the note from that guy, Kevin Cravens. Then, Meredith took Emily, and I went back to the Red Lion Inn to take a shower and a nap. I was so exhausted I didn't even worry too much about the ghost in the closet. I just laid down on the bed and fell asleep, and now... here I am. Wearing the same clothes I went to sleep in!

Which consists of nothing more than a short t-shirt and some bikini panties.

"You could at least get me a robe," Melody said, her face now beet red, as she tried to make sure her panties were covered by her t-shirt.

"No prob," JD said easily. He walked to her bathroom, took the robe from the hook on the back of the door, and handed it to her.

"I wish you had given me a chance to say good-bye to Emily and Meredith," Melody said, tying the sash on her robe.

"Tell 'em yourself," JD said.

"My mission's not over?" Melody asked, confused. "I felt sure that now—"

"Unplanned interruption, that Cravens jerk," JD said. "Bogus dude, huh?"

"Didn't you know he was coming?" Melody asked.

"Hey, do I look like the Big Guy to you?" JD asked, folding his arms.

"How would I know?" Melody said. "I have no idea what the Big Guy looks like."

"Good point. Score one for you," JD said, nodding. "Anyway, the answer to your question is no, I did not know Payton Fire was going to go after Emily."

Melody's eyes grew wide. "You mean Kevin Cravens is really—"

"Bingo," JD said. "Not that Payton is really Payton, either. Those Deep Sixers don't actually look human at all—"

"I know," Melody said with a shudder. "I got a brief glimpse."

"Oh yeah, when ol' Kev got ticked off. Yeah, they lose some control over their physical form when they get really mad. Good thing to remember when you're on assignment."

"I will," Melody promised.

"Any-hoo," JD continued, "I can't anticipate everything. And you've got another day Down Below, till Tarshea takes her test."

"Okay," Melody said. She yawned. She really was exhausted.

"You did good," JD confirmed. "Real good. I'll show you in a minute."

"Hey, I just realized . . . where is everyone?" Melody asked, realizing that the entire dorm was quiet. Usually, at least some of the kids had their sound systems cranked up, or their radios tuned to one of the many Teen Heaven radio stations.

"School, natch," JD said. "It's just the middle of the afternoon here."

Melody put her hand to her head. "It's all so confusing sometimes..."

"Yeah, well, that's life!" JD said with a laugh.

"Hey, Melody, far-out!" Free said, sticking her head into the room. Her frizzy hair stuck straight out from beneath a headband embroidered with peace symbols that encircled her forehead.

"Hi, Free," Melody said.

Free took in Melody's cut-up and bruised shins beneath the hem of her knee-length robe. "Whoa, bummer. How'd you do that?"

"Down Below," Melody said. "I'm in the middle of an assignment."

"Yeah, JD told me," Free said. "Want me to make you a cup of herbal tea?"

"I'd love a—" Melody began.

"Sorry, Free, no time," JD said. "She's going back down."

"Major drag," Free said. She walked over to Melody and gave her a hug. "We miss you up here. Come home soon."

"Thanks, Free," Melody said, hugging the young African-American woman back. "I miss everyone, too."

"Hang in," Free said, flipping Melody the peace symbol. "You can do it." Free padded out of the room, her patchouli oil scent wafting behind her.

"I love her," Melody said in a small, shy voice.

"Yeah, Free is majorly cool," JD agreed. "So, where was I? Oh yeah, school. You keeping up on your homework?"

Melody sighed.

"Don't get behind," JD counseled her, picking up one of Nicole's pencils and balancing it neatly in his palm on its eraser. "You got Capelli for English, right?"

Melody nodded.

"The dude will toast you if you don't keep up," JD said. He flipped the pencil back to the desk. "So listen, you get dressed, I'll meet you right outside. I want to show you something."

Instead of disappearing, JD just strolled out the door of Melody's room, and closed the door behind him. For a quick minute, Melody luxuriated in the feeling of being in her own room, in her own bed, with no terrifying creatures from Deep Six to frighten her, and no ghost in room 20 to give her sleepless nights.

"I'm waiting!" JD called from outside the door.

"Coming," Melody called back. She quickly pulled on some jeans and a pink sweatshirt that read "Teen Angels Are Among Us," then she went outside to meet JD.

"Cool sweatshirt," JD said. He snapped his fingers once, and Melody found herself in one of the comfortable theater chairs in the Center of Everything, facing the EarthScope, JD a couple of chairs away.

"Let's go to the videotape!" JD called.

Instantly, the room darkened, the screen glowed purple, and then it lit up.

Melody gasped, involuntarily.

Because there she was, outside the Happy Days Daycare Center, holding Emily's hand.

And she was wearing the same clothes she had

been wearing just a few hours before.

"Is that really me?" she asked JD.

"That's you," JD agreed. "Well, it was you, but let's not get technical. Let's check out your performance."

Melody watched, absolutely dumbfounded, as the EarthScope played out the beginning of her horrible encounter with Kevin Cravens.

Then, she saw Kevin Cravens grab Emily away from her, and she saw herself, on the screen, standing stock-still, unable to move. She felt as if she were reliving the horror of it all over again. Her mouth was dry, her heart was racing and she felt barely able to speak.

"JD..." Melody managed to squeak out.

Instantly, the picture on the EarthScope stopped, as if it really were a videotape.

"Yeah," JD asked, turning to her.

"Right here," Melody said, feeling the same fear well up in her that she'd felt when she was Down Below, "I felt like I couldn't move. Like I was frozen."

"You are frozen," JD acknowledged. "The tape is stopped."

"I mean in real life!" Melody hastened to explain. "Was anything holding me there? I mean, was the guy from Deep Six doing that to me?"

JD wrinkled his brow. "Naaaah. At least I don't think so. It would sure be a new one on me," he admitted. "I'll ask the Big Guy about it, if that'll help."

"Because I felt sure..." Melody said softly. "And then, well, can you put the tape back on?"

Instantly, the tape started moving forward again.

"There you go," JD said approvingly, watching Melody take off on the screen after Kevin, "just as if you played football for the Fortyniners or something."

"Stop it again!" Melody asserted.

The tape stopped.

"And just before that," Melody said, "I heard someone talking to me."

"Oh?" JD asked, his voice quizzical. "I don't see anyone else on the screen."

"I heard a voice," Melody maintained. "It told me I had to do something, that I had the power. So, what was it?"

"Beats me," JD said, taking out his ever-present little notebook from his back pocket.

"Disembodied voices, Stockbridge, Massachusetts," he continued, jotting some notes down. "I'll get it checked out."

"Someone was there," Melody said firmly.

"*You* were there," JD pointed out.

Melody sighed. *I don't think I'm being very convincing,* she thought. *I don't think JD believes me about the voice.*

"So," JD, said, "let's cut to the chase, so to speak. Geez, I slay me sometimes." The videotape sped up, faster and faster, until the moment of truth, when Melody made her flying open field tackle of Emily.

"Awesome," JD said, giving the high five to the ceiling.

CRACK!

Something made the slapping sound of high five against his hand, although there was no one else in the Center of Everything.

Melody shook her head. *This is a very strange place*, she thought. *Very, very strange.*

"No penalty markers on the play," JD commented wryly on Melody's tackle, as if it were *Monday Night Football*. "And the Angels take over on downs!"

Melody smiled shyly. "I'm glad I saved her," she said.

JD leaned back and roared with laughter. "Glad?" he said. "Glad? Melody, babe, kindly tender me your Angel Card."

Melody reached into her purse and took out her ever-present Angel Card. She handed it to JD.

"Melody Monroe," JD said, standing up and walking over to the bank-teller-like machine on the far wall, "the last time I awarded someone interim Angel Points in the midst of an uncompleted mission was in . . . well, a long time ago." He stuck Melody's card in the machine.

"TWO THOUSAND POINTS," the machine intoned. "TWO THOUSAND POINTS CREDITED MELODY MONROE."

"Wow," Melody breathed. "You just gave me—?"

"Yeah," JD confirmed. "Now, get your homework done and finish your mission," JD said kindly from where he stood across the room, snapping the Angel Card toward Melody like a Frisbee. It flew toward her, and dropped directly at her feet, floating down as if it were as light as a feather.

"Amazing," Melody breathed.

"Practice," JD said proudly. "So, anything else?"

"Excuse me?" Melody asked, not comprehending.

"Any other requests, before you get sent back down?" JD said, walking toward her.

Melody thought a moment. "Can I go back to my room?" she asked shyly. "I think I might have forgotten one of the books for Mr. Capelli's class."

"Wise idea," JD said slyly. "Well, see you soon!"

JD snapped his fingers, and Melody was back in her room.

I really did forget one of the books for English, she thought, going over to her desk and picking up the book. *I really wish Cisco and Nicole were here. And I miss Chaz, I miss him so much...*

Chaz. She sat on her bed, lost in thought, hugging her English book to her. *I can't believe he was with Scarlett Whitmore. But I'm sure they're in school, and—*

Someone knocked at the door of Melody's room.

Melody's heart leapt. Maybe it was Chaz. She ran over to open it.

Celeste Durkey barged into the room.

"I heard noises in here, so I thought I'd investigate," Celeste said proudly, making a beeline for Melody's bed and plopping herself right down on it. She was wearing a typical Celeste Durkey outfit—pink shorts with purple polkadots on them, and a pink t-shirt with purple and green glittery angels flying around. Her high-top pink sneakers featured glittery purple and green shoelaces.

"Hello, Celeste," Melody said politely.

"What are you doing here?" Celeste demanded. "I thought you were Down Below. Did you fail? Your mission? I've never failed a mission."

"No," Melody said politely, "I didn't fail. What are you doing here?"

"I told you," Celeste said, lying down on Melody's bed as if it were her own. She crossed her arms under her head, making herself comfortable. "Investigating."

"Don't you have class?" Melody asked her.

"I do, but it's last period and Miss Robbins let me out because I did all my homework," Celeste smiled with satisfaction. "And all my homework for next week, and the week afterward. And don't bother to ask if you can copy, because the answer is *N-O*, no."

"I didn't ask," Melody pointed out. Now that she had her book, she expected to be beamed down at any moment, back to Stockbridge. And she did not relish the idea of leaving Celeste Durkey alone, unattended, in her room.

"I think we should go now," Melody continued.

"But why?" Celeste whined. "I like it here."

"Because I'm going to be sent back Down Below," Melody said assertively.

"But—"

"Celeste," Melody said, "let's go. Okay?"

Celeste made a gigantic shrug, and got up from Melody's bed. Together, they left Melody's room.

JD was standing outside, leaning against the wall, sucking on a Tootsie-pop. He looked as gorgeous as ever.

"Hello ladies," he said easily. "Melody, you ready to boogie?"

"If you want to send me Down Below to help her, you can," Celeste offered.

"Gee, Celeste, real kind of you," JD said. "But Mel's got this one under control."

"Well, okay then," Celeste said with a shrug. "I'll be seeing you." She made no move to leave.

"Hey, what say we go downstairs, get one more good breath of heavenly air, okay?" JD suggested.

"Sure," Melody agreed.

"What about me?" Celeste asked eagerly.

"Don't you have homework?" JD asked hopefully.

"Nope!" Celeste cried. "I did it all! I always do it all. If you want to come check it, you can, because—"

"Zip it, Celeste," JD suggested.

"Zip it, right," Celeste agreed. She pulled an imaginary zipper across her mouth and then pretended to throw away the key.

"Just one good breath of Teen Heaven air, and you're on your way," JD said, his arm around Melody as he led her toward the front door of the dorm.

They stepped outside.

"Oh, no!" Melody cried, tears coming to her eyes.

Because what she saw coming her way made her feel sick and sad and like she'd been punched in the stomach, all at the same time.

Eleven

Melody sucked in her breath so hard it sounded like a shriek. Because coming toward her was Chaz. With Scarlett.

And they totally looked as if they belonged together, a happy couple. In love.

"Oh, look who's here," JD said easily, nodding his head at Chaz and Scarlett. They strolled over, laughing and talking in low, intimate tones.

"Hi, Mel!" Chaz said, a huge grin on his face. "Scarlett just told me the funniest story about what happened to her today in English..."

"Who cares?" Melody practically shouted.

"Mel—" Chaz began, taken aback.

"No, don't 'Mel' me!" Melody exploded. "Every time I show up here unexpectedly the two of you are together!"

"Why, Melody, whatever do you mean?" Scarlett asked, confusion furrowing her perfect brow.

"I mean, I mean...I don't know what I mean," Melody admitted. She was so embarrassed that she felt as if she could drop through the ground, all the way down to Deep Six.

"You're not jealous, are you?" Scarlett asked, wide-eyed.

"Why, should I be?" Melody asked, jutting her chin forward.

"Jealousy is such a nasty little emotion," Scarlett said. "Have you ever noticed how it can make a really, really pretty girl look really, really ugly?"

"You ought to know," Melody snapped.

"Hey, you guys, come on—" Chaz chided them.

"Uh, excuse me for breaking up this little teen crisis," JD said, staring at Melody, "but might I remind you that you are a Teen Angel in the middle of a mission. And that mission is Down Below, babe."

Melody bit her lower lip with chagrin. "I know, you're right—"

"I can't believe you don't trust me," Chaz said, a hurt look in his eyes.

Melody felt terrible. Her stomach hurt and her heart ached. *Oh, Chaz, I love you so much*, she thought to herself. *How can you betray me, with Scarlett Whitmore, of all people? How?*

But she knew she couldn't say those things. She didn't have the nerve. And after all, Chaz had never said he wouldn't date any other girls.

I guess he doesn't care about me as much as I thought, Melody realized. *Out of sight, out of mind.*

"Listen, Mel—" Chaz began, reaching for her arm, but she shook him off.

"I'm in the middle of a mission," she said tersely. "I have to go."

Scarlett nodded. "We understand." She slipped her arm through Chaz's and snuggled close. "Too bad you won't be around tonight," she told Melody. "We're going on a moonlight hayride. All your friends are going. Well, I guess I should say *my* friends now. Right, Chaz?"

"We're *all* friends," Chaz said easily.

Is that all I am to you? Melody wondered.

"That sounds like fun," Melody said, forcing her voice to sound unemotional. She turned away from Chaz and Scarlett. "Beam me back down," she told JD, gulping hard. "I have work to do."

"I still can't believe someone tried to snatch Emily," Meredith said, as she handed Melody a glass of cider.

It was a couple of hours later. JD had beamed Melody back down to the Red Lion Inn, and Melody was sitting on the front porch, in her favorite rocker, trying to keep her mind on her mission instead of obsessing about Chaz and Scarlett.

What's wrong with you, Melody? she asked herself. *Here you are with some terrible changeling from Deep Six who's coming after you and Emily, and all you can think about is your own stupid romance in Teen Heaven.*

She forced her thoughts back down to Earth. "I know, it's terrible," Melody agreed, taking a sip of her drink.

"You know what really has me freaked out?" Meredith asked, leaning close. "You said that the guy who tried to snatch Emily knew her name, and my name, and your name. He knew where I worked. Now, how did he get all the information?"

He got it from the Bad Dude in Deep Six, Melody

longed to say, but of course she knew she couldn't.

"I mean, this is not just some random sicko," Meredith continued, her voice tense with worry. "This is someone who, like, *studied* us."

"I promise you I'll watch over Emily," Melody said.

"At least I know she's safe right now," Meredith said. "I'm glad Mom kept her at her office with her tonight. But she can't do that all the time!"

"I won't let her out of my sight at the daycare center tomorrow," Melody said.

"Mom wants to keep her home," Meredith said, her voice etched with anxiety, "but her boss is already on the warpath because she was out so much last month when Emily had the flu and then the chicken pox. And Mom can't afford to lose her job."

"Tomorrow, have your mom deliver Emily directly to me," Melody said. "Okay?"

"Okay," Meredith said, but she didn't sound convinced. She fiddled nervously with the slender chain around her neck. "If anything happened to Emily, I don't know what I would do..."

"Nothing's going to happen to her," Melody said.

"You don't know that," Meredith said sharply.

Melody reached out to touch Meredith's hand. "I know that powerful forces are watching over her."

"What are you talking about?" Meredith asked.

"Never mind," Melody said. "I . . . I can't really explain."

Meredith shook her head. "Boy, you think that you live in a safe place, far from the big city . . ." Her lip trembled. "Now no place feels safe to me. I really, really hate it."

"Miss! I asked for a cup of coffee!" a man bellowed from across the porch.

"I'd better get to work before I lose my job," Meredith said.

"What time do you get off?" Melody asked.

Meredith checked her watch. "In forty-five minutes. Forty-five really, really long minutes."

"Why don't we get some cold drinks and go hang out in my room when you get off?" Melody suggested impetuously. *Wow,* she thought to herself happily. *That was so very assertive of me!*

"Gee, I don't know—" Meredith began.

"Oh, it's okay," Melody said, quickly backing down. "I'm sure you have other plans—"

"No, I don't," Meredith said. "I'm just concerned about Emily—"

"We can call her from my room," Melody suggested. Then she grinned. "Unless you're afraid of the ghost in my closet, that is."

Meredith grinned. "Oh, well, we'll be together. How much damage can the ghost do?"

"Exactly," Melody agreed.

"Miss, the coffee?"

"Right away, sir," Meredith called. She smiled at Melody. "See you in forty-three minutes."

"Oh, this is heavenly," Meredith said, collapsing onto Melody's bed in room 20. "My feet are killing me." She swung her body around on the bed and put her feet up high on the wall. "Ahhhh, much better."

Melody took in her strange position, and laughed.

"Hey, don't laugh, it works!" Meredith said. "If you put your feet higher than your head, all the blood rushes out of them or something. Is it okay if I use your phone?"

Melody handed it to her, and Meredith quickly dialed her home number. "Hi, Mom," Melody heard Meredith say. Meredith quickly explained that she was in Melody's room at the Inn. Then she listened for a long time.

"That's fantastic!" she cried. "Let me tell Melody!" She took her mouth from the phone. "Mel, the police caught the guy who tried to snatch Emily!"

"That's great!" Melody said automatically, but her mind was in turmoil. *How could they have caught him? He doesn't really exist!* "Where did they find him?"

Meredith listened to her mom for a few more moments. "Mom says they got a tip from someone who said he knew a guy who matched the description you gave the police. They caught him at home and took him into the police station. Can you imagine? He's in custody now."

She put her ear back to the phone. "Uh huh ... uh huh ... I'll ask her." She turned to Melody. "They want to know if you can go down to the police station in an hour, to identify him."

"Sure," Melody said.

"She said sure," Meredith told her mom. "Oh, I am so relieved! Put Emily on the phone." Meredith turned to Melody. "Isn't this fantastic?"

"It really is," Melody agreed, even though how she really felt was both wary and confused.

"Hi, cutie!" Meredith said gaily to her little sister. "You okay? They got that bad guy, so you don't have to worry about anything anymore. Melody and I both send you lots of kisses . . . night!" Meredith hung up, swinging around on the bed, her eyes shining. "I can't even begin to tell you how much better I feel!"

"It's really wonderful," Melody said, sipping the Diet Coke she'd brought upstairs with her.

"Maybe now we'll find out who this sicko really is," Meredith said.

I know who he is, Melody thought, *what I don't know is why he let himself get caught*. But she didn't say that, she just sipped her Coke.

"So, now that I know my little sister is safe from the loony-tune, let's talk about something totally different," Meredith decided. "Like guys. Do you have a boyfriend?"

Melody shrugged.

"What am I saying?" Meredith continued, hitting herself in the head. "Look at you! Of course you have a boyfriend! I cannot imagine what it must be like to be as gorgeous as you are."

"I don't feel very gorgeous most of the time," Melody said in a small voice.

"You're kidding," Meredith said.

Melody shook her head. "Silly, isn't it?"

"Yes, as a matter of fact, it is," Meredith said. "I mean, I know I'm nice-looking, maybe even pretty, but you . . . you're, like, out of this world!"

Exactly, Melody thought, *but not in the way you mean*. She took another sip of her Coke. "Right now I'm having some guy problems," she admitted.

"You?" Meredith asked, reaching for her drink. "I find that hard to believe."

"It's true," Melody said. "I have a boyfriend—or at least I thought I did. His name is Chaz. And lately he's been hanging out with this girl who I know is after him, but he claims they're just friends."

"Maybe they really are just friends," Meredith said.

"No," Melody said firmly. "I can see right through her. She wants him and now I think she's got him. And everyone just thinks I'm being jealous." She sighed. "Oh, who knows, maybe I am. Anyway, she's up there and I'm down here..."

"Where's up there?" Meredith asked.

"What?"

"You said 'she's up there, and I'm down here...'"

"Oh," Melody said, her heart beating quickly. "I meant... uh... Maine!" she invented quickly, trying to remember from a long-ago junior high geography class what state would be "up" from Massachusetts.

"You're from Maine?" Meredith asked.

"No, but this girl is... uh... in Maine," Melody improvised. "And so is my boyfriend."

Meredith looked skeptical. "So what are they doing in Maine?"

"Uh... you know..." Melody said, since she felt horrible about making up any more lies. *And I'm not very good at it, either*, she thought. *This is what I get for confiding my Teen Heaven problems to an earthling!*

"There's a guy I like," Meredith said, evidently willing to let Melody's strange story slide.

"Who?" Melody asked eagerly, happy not to have to tell any more lies.

"He goes to North, which is the high school on the other side of town," Meredith said. "I did some volunteer work for the Special Olympics and I met him there. He's really nice, and cute, and smart. In fact, he's famous. Really, really, really famous. He's got his own TV series. His name is Joey Lawrence."

Melody's jaw dropped. "Wait a second. Do you mean the Joey Lawrence on TV? The cute guy with the dark hair?"

"Exactly," Meredith said.

"And you're telling me he goes to North Berkshire High School?" Melody asked slowly.

"Uh huh," Meredith said, sipping her Coke. "You believe me, don't you?"

"Honestly, no," Melody said. "I don't believe you at all."

"Well, good," Meredith replied, laughing. "Because that's just about how much I believe that story about your boyfriend and some girl in Maine—"

"OO-oo-oo-oo-ooo!"

The sound came from the closet, and both girls jumped from fright.

"Wh—what was that?" Meredith asked, gulping hard.

"The ghost," Melody whispered, staring hard at the closet.

"But it can't be!" Meredith said, her voice trembling.

"But it is," Melody insisted. "You're the one who told me the room is haunted!"

"But that was just a joke!" Meredith insisted.

"Oo-oo-oo-oooooo!"

"Oh, God, something is really in the closet," Meredith said, clutching the pillow on the bed to her chest.

"What do you mean, 'it was just a joke'?" Melody asked, her eyes glued to the closet.

"I mean that I was just teasing you," Meredith said. "I don't even believe in ghosts!"

"Well, who do you think is in my closet moaning?" Melody whispered frantically. "I heard him last night, too."

"I know, but last night—"

"OO-oo-oo-oo-oo! Oo-oo-oo-oo!" The closet door vibrated and the girls screamed in fright.

"There really is a ghost!" Melody gasped. "Do you think it's evil?"

"What I think is that I'm going crazy!" Meredith blurted out.

"No, you're not," Melody assured her. "I hear it, too. Believe me, last night when I was in here alone and the moaning started, I thought *I* was the one going crazy!"

"But you weren't alone!" Meredith said.

"Yes, I was," Melody insisted. "Just me and that ghost—"

"It wasn't a ghost!" Meredith cried.

"What do you mean?"

"I mean it was me!" Meredith admitted. "There's a passage in the back of that closet to the storage room."

"You mean you—"

"I made those noises last night," Meredith admitted. "It was just a joke!"

"I'm not laughing!" Melody said. "You scared the life out of me!"

"Oo-oo-oo-oo-oo! Oo-oo-oo-oo-oo! Oo-oo-oo-oo-oo!"

Both girls screamed again.

"This isn't funny!" Melody cried.

"I know that now!" Meredith yelled. "Because if I'm not in there moaning and shaking the door, who is?"

Twelve

"OOO-oooo!" came the noise from the closet again.

Meredith shrieked and clutched Melody's arm in abject terror.

"It's true, you know," Meredith gasped.

"What's true?" Melody whispered back, her eyes still glued to the closet door.

Please let it be over, she thought to herself. *Please let that be the end of it. No more ghost noises. I hope...*

"The story about the violinist," Meredith said, gulping so loud that Melody could actually hear her swallow. "He really did kill himself in this room."

"Oh, terrific," Melody replied.

"But the rest of it, about the room being haunted and everything, that's just a silly story—"

"OOOOO-ooooo!"

The noise was back.

"Oh, really?" Melody asked. "Tell that to the ghost making those terrible noises in my closet!"

"I don't believe in ghosts," Meredith chanted,

"I don't, I don't, I don't believe in ghosts . . ."

"Ooooo-oooooooooo!"

"I say we make a run for it!" Meredith gasped, but she was too petrified by fear to move a muscle.

Melody steeled herself. *I took on that guy from Deep Six*, she told herself. *I am a Teen Angel. I am not going to let some scary—*

"OOOOOO-ooooo! Ha-ha-ha-ha-haaaaaa!"

The scary sound from the closet turned into a sick, evil laugh, a laugh that reminded Melody of the laugh that Kevin Cravens had cackled as he ran away with Emily.

It can't be him, Melody thought. And then she changed her mind. *Why not? Of course it can be him. Do you really think that a changeling from Deep Six could be in police custody, you idiot?*

"When that violinist killed himself," Meredith began, her teeth chattering with fear, "it . . . it was so bloody. They put the pictures in the paper."

"I'm going to open the door," Melody said, making a decision.

"Noooo!" Meredith yelped. "You can't!"

"OOOOOO-ooooo!" came the sound from the closet, louder than before. Melody and Meredith both jumped again.

"See, you're making him mad!" Meredith screamed. "He doesn't want you to open the door!"

"But I am," Melody insisted. And even though she was so scared she thought she could die all over again from the fright she felt, she got up from the bed, her knees quivering from fear, perspiration pouring down her arms, her teeth nearly chattering, and she slowly headed for the closet door.

I'm scared, she told herself. *But I am opening that door. Right now. I am a Teen Angel. I am strong. I have faith. I can do this.*

She forced herself to walk over to the closet. Just before she put her sweaty hand on the doorknob, she took one look back at Meredith. The girl had her arms wrapped around herself, hugging her body, her eyes screwed absolutely shut.

Melody put her hand on the doorknob.

"OOOOO-ooooo! Ha-ha-ha-ha-ha-ha-haaaaa!"

She gave the knob a quick twist and opened the door.

And looked into ...

Nothing.

Except her clothes.

She looked down. And there on a milk crate, just behind her clothes, was a portable cassette recorder.

Melody instantly reached down and picked it up, and snapped it off.

It was a small, black, battery-operated cassette recorder, attached to some kind of crude timing device. She turned and showed it to Meredith.

"That's it?" Meredith asked, astonished, taking her hands away from her body. "That's our ghost?"

Melody pushed the "on" button on the cassette player. Instantly, the horrible moaning and laughing filled the room again.

Meredith started to giggle. So did Melody. And then, the two of them were laughing as hard as they could together.

Melody pushed her clothes aside and looked further into the closet. And she found a metal pole hooked up to a motor and battery in a box, the pole leaning against the bottom of the door. When the box vibrated, so did the door.

"Look at this!" Melody cried, and Meredith hurried over to the closet.

"Wow, what a setup!" Meredith gasped. "It's much better than mine."

"I still can't believe you scared me on purpose," Melody said, examining the closet even further.

"It wasn't even a little funny?" Meredith asked.

"A little," Melody admitted. "Now that I know some horrible monster isn't back here. So, who do you think did this?" She put her head back into the closet, searching for clues. "Hey, I found something!"

"What is it?" Meredith asked eagerly.

Back where she'd found the cassette player, Melody found a small white envelope. When she picked it up and looked at it, she saw written on the outside of it: TO MY DEAR MELODY.

"Whoever this is from knows your name," Meredith pointed out. She thought a moment. "Oh, no, not Kevin—"

Believe me, Deep Sixers pull stunts much scarier than this, Melody wanted to say, but of course she couldn't. So instead she just opened the note.

It was short, handwritten, and to the point.

Dear Melody—

Boo.

Dr. Frazier

"Did you know about this?" Melody demanded.

"Nope, I swear I didn't," Meredith answered, starting to giggle again. "Do you think I could have faked how frightened I was?"

"Yes," Melody said softly. Then she started to giggle, too. And then, both of them were consumed with laughter once again.

"But... I do have another confession to make," Meredith said, as she tried to get her breath.

"I'm afraid to hear it," Melody said, through her laughter.

"Well, Dr. Frazier isn't really Dr. Frazier," she admitted with chagrin.

"Who is he, then?" Melody asked.

"My Uncle Louie," Meredith said. "It's a joke we pull on people who are staying in room twenty, you know, that whole thing about how he's this parapsychologist—"

"You mean he isn't really?" Melody asked.

Meredith shook her head. "He owns a hardware store in Housatonic."

"Oh, that's just great," Melody said, her hands on her hips. "And the two of you thought it was sooo funny..."

"Well, yeah," Meredith admitted, biting her lip to keep from laughing. "We kinda did."

Melody couldn't help it—she burst out laughing again, and Meredith joined in. "It looks like 'Dr. Frazier' has taken his haunting one step further without your help," Melody said.

Meredith nodded in agreement. "Uncle Louie just loves practical jokes," she said. "I just never thought the joke would end up on me!"

* * *

"Back again," Meredith said an hour later, as she and Melody walked through the parking lot that approached the tiny Stockbridge town police department. "I am so happy they caught that scum, aren't you?"

"Sure," Melody agreed, even though deep down she wondered how it could be possible that the police had managed to catch a guy from Deep Six.

"So, all you have to do is ID the guy, I guess."

"I guess," Melody said, keeping pace with Meredith.

"Then, no problem," Meredith responded, bounding up the two steps that led to the police department entrance. "I hope he goes to prison for a really long time for scaring my sister like that."

Melody followed her, her head full of confused thoughts.

Could I be wrong about the guy being from Deep Six?

If he was from Deep Six, how could he have been caught? And what if there's a trial? Will I have to testify?

What if they find out I'm really dead?

And then she always came back to the same thought: *no way would a Deep Sixer let himself get caught by the police . . .*

With false confidence, Melody approached the handsome, overweight policeman who was sitting behind the desk. It was a different cop from the one to whom she'd earlier given her statement, but Melody recognized him as the same policeman whom she'd seen directing traffic on

Main Street her first day in Stockbridge.

His head was buried in a newspaper.

"I'm Melody Monroe," she said quietly, not wanting to startle him. "I'm here to identify Kevin Cravens."

The policeman startled anyway, putting the newspaper away guiltily and jumping to his feet.

"Miss Monroe, of course," he said with exaggerated politeness. "Well, this should be a slam dunk."

"Excuse me?" Melody asked.

"Easiest ID in history," said the policeman, whose name badge identified him as Officer Ropalinsky. "I'm Ropalinsky. Just call me Officer Ropie, okay?"

"Okay," Melody said.

"Weird, though," Officer Ropie said. "The kid swears he wasn't there."

"Maybe it's not the right person—" Melody began tentatively.

"I'm so sure," Meredith snorted angrily. "He was there, all right."

"Well, this kid's name is Kevin Cravens, so it all checks out. Why don't you girls have a seat," Officer Ropie said, "and we'll bring him out. He's in the lockup in the back."

Melody and Meredith went to sit down in the two metal folding chairs that were across from Officer Ropie's small desk.

"It would be terrible if they have the wrong person," Melody said nervously.

"How many Kevin Cravenses do you think there are in this part of Massachusetts?" Meredith asked. "It's got to be the same guy."

At that moment, two cops—Officer Ropie and

another short, slender guy with red hair—walked over to Melody and Meredith. Between them was a very-scared-looking eighteen-year-old kid whom they held by the arms.

Not that they needed to. His wrists were handcuffed behind him. And he didn't look ready to run anywhere.

"This the perp?" Officer Ropie asked Melody.

"Perp?" Melody echoed.

"Perpetrator," Officer Ropie explained. "They guy who did it. One Kevin Cravens."

Melody got a sick feeling in her stomach again.

It was him. The guy had the same brown hair that fell over his forehead, the same muscular build. Melody even thought that she recognized the Nikes he was wearing.

And then Melody steeled herself, knowing what she had to do.

She had to look directly into his eyes.

She raised her head and made eye contact with Kevin.

He had pupils. Normal blue eyes, with normal dark pupils.

Just like any other normal human.

"So, miss," Officer Ropie prompted her, "is this the guy?"

"I...I..." Melody stammered, not knowing what to do or say.

"It checks out," the redheaded officer said. "He's Kevin Cravens, from Pittsfield. There's only one."

"Look, I told you guys, I was at an Eagle Scout meeting!" Kevin exclaimed, his eyes wide with fright. "I didn't do this!"

"Kindly shut up," Office Ropie said to the guy.

"So?" the redheaded cop asked again, "is this the guy?"

Melody panicked.

It is him! she thought. *But it isn't him! Do you think that—*

At that moment, the door to the police station burst open.

The two cops, momentarily startled, left their hands free to reach for their guns if necessary.

But it was not exactly criminals who entered the police station. It was a group of seven Eagle Scouts, plus two adult scoutmasters, all of them still in uniform, who had burst through the door.

"Kevin!" one of the teen boys shouted, rushing over to him.

"What the heck is going on here?" one of the the adult scoutmasters demanded.

"We got a call from your mom, Kevin," the other scoutmaster explained. "She told us some crazy story about you being arrested for kidnapping—"

"Attempted kidnapping," Officer Ropie explained. "And we already offered for Kevin here to call his attorney. He declined."

"Because I didn't do anything!" Kevin implored. "Mr. Sanders, please, tell 'em where I was!"

"Officers," the scoutmaster said, "I'm Jonathan Sanders, Kevin's scoutmaster. This boy was with us for the entire afternoon."

"We swear it!" one of the Eagle Scouts said. "Scouts honor!"

All the other Eagle Scouts nodded affirmatively.

"It's true," one of them declared.

The two police officers looked at each other, puzzled.

"Miss," Officer Ropie said, turning to Melody, "it's up to you. You ID the guy, we hold him. If not, we'll let him go."

"He's the guy!" Meredith declared. "I know it!"

Melody closed her eyes to think. Then, she opened them, and carefully scrutinized each of the Eagle Scouts and their scoutmasters.

They all had pupils.

I know the guy who grabbed Emily had no pupils, Melody thought decisively. *I just know it. I'm not making a mistake. That was a Deep Six Kevin, and this is a human Kevin.*

I think. I hope.

"He looks like the guy I saw," Melody began slowly. "And he used the same name as him—"

"Then, that settles it," the other cop said. "We're holding him—"

"—but it's not the same guy," Melody said, finishing her sentence.

"What?" Meredith said, stunned.

"It's not the same guy," Melody repeated. "You've got to let him go."

"Miss, are you sure?" Officer Ropie asked.

"I'm sure," Melody insisted. "This is not the same person who tried to kidnap Emily."

"But—" Meredith protested.

"I'm sorry," Melody told her. "I know you want it to be the same person. And so do I. But it just . . . isn't."

The two cops looked at each other and shrugged. Then, slowly, they reached behind Kevin Cravens, who was looking at Melody with pupils wide, his eyes full of gratitude. There was a slow click, and Kevin's handcuffs were gone.

"How can I ever thank you?" Kevin said to Melody, rubbing his wrists.

"You don't have to," Melody replied softly. "I'm just glad I could do the right thing."

Meredith had tears in her eyes. "Maybe you did do the right thing," she said. "You seem to be certain it's not the same guy. But Melody, that means he's out there. The guy who tried to kidnap Emily is still out there. Which means next time, he could succeed."

My last day, Melody thought happily, as she opened the front door of Happy Days Daycare to admit a gaggle of kids who all seemed to have been dropped off by their parents at once. *My last day, and then back to Teen Heaven, to my friends and to . . . Chaz.*

Melody's eyes clouded when she thought of Chaz. The thought of Chaz together with Scarlett Whitmore was almost too much to bear.

Let's face it, I'm no match for her, Melody thought. It looks like she's won . . .

"Melody, play with me!"

"No, me!"

"No, me!"

"No, I asked her first!"

"Please?"

"Pretty please?"

"Pretty please with sugar on top?"

"Shut up, you doody-bomb! I asked first!"

Of course, I could just stay here forever with the Doody-Bomb Kid, Melody thought to herself, looking over her brood. *I have to say I have a new appreciation for anyone who works in daycare!* She turned to embrace each one of the kids, and all the three- and four-year-olds gathered around her, eager for her love and affection.

I wonder what happens to little kids when they die, she mused. *Maybe there's a Baby Heaven. I'll have to ask JD.*

From behind her, she heard a loud crash, and nearly jumped out of her skin.

"Sorry," Mrs. Plant called from the kitchen area, "I dropped a glass."

I'm still nervous about the Deep Sixers, Melody realized. *They may have failed with Emily, but that doesn't mean they won't try again . . .*

Stockbridge was not the safe little New England village that it appeared to be. Not at all.

And there was no one Melody could tell about it. Not here, Down Below, anyway.

There was a rap at the front door of the daycare center.

Someone's late, Melody thought.

"I'll get it," she called out to Mrs. Plant, removing the Doody-Bomb Kid from his death-grip of her right leg. "I'll be right back," she promised him.

"Can I come?" Emily asked. Ever since she'd arrived that morning, she'd stuck to Melody like a shadow.

"Sure," Melody said, understanding that the little girl now felt very scared and insecure.

"Hey, how come her and not me?" the Doody-Bomb Kid yelled. "No fair!"

"You'll get to start the next game, how's that?" Melody said, as she and Emily walked hand-in-hand to the front door.

She opened it. And what she saw tore a scream from her throat.

Because no one was there.

But a pickup truck had veered off the street, and it was heading straight up the path, directly toward her and Emily.

And there was no driver behind the wheel.

Thirteen

For the briefest moment, a fraction of a second, Melody was overcome once again with that same terrible feeling that had kept her glued to the spot, unable to move, unable to run after Kevin when he snatched Emily.

And in the next fraction of a second, Melody heard the same strong, soothing voice that had spoken to her before:

"You are a Teen Angel," it said. "You have the power."

"Everybody, run!" was all Melody had time to say, as she threw her body into Emily's like the last time, only this time she rolled with the tiny girl, over and over, out of the way of the oncoming pickup truck.

In the next instant, the pickup truck crashed through the front door of the daycare center, where it abruptly came to a screeching stop, as if someone were pressing hard on the brakes.

The only sound in the room was that of little children crying and whimpering.

"Children, are you all right?" Mrs. Plant

called, standing up, her legs none too steady. "Is anyone hurt?"

No one replied.

Melody looked down at Emily, who was still wedged partly underneath her. "You okay?"

Emily nodded, but her face was the color of milk, and she was trembling all over. Melody gave her a quick hug, then she stood up. Her own legs felt like overcooked spaghetti.

Slowly she walked over to the truck, to make certain that no little kids were—God forbid—caught underneath it.

"I think everyone is safe," Melody called to Mrs. Plant.

"Quickly, children," Mrs. Plant called out to them, "form a line over here by me so that I can check and make sure everyone is accounted for."

Emily ran over to Melody and threw her arms around her.

"It's okay, Emily," Melody said in a soothing voice. "You can go over by Mrs. Plant."

"No!" Emily cried, tears streaming down her face.

"I'll go with you," Melody said, taking the little girl's hand. She walked Emily over to the group, where Mrs. Plant checked all the kids off her list.

"Yes, we're all here and we're all fine," Mrs. Plant said, relief coloring her voice. She looked over at the pickup truck, so incongruous-looking inside the daycare. "I'm calling the police."

"I wanna go home!" the Doody-Bomb Kid cried, burying his head in his hands.

"Me, too!" another child yelled.

"Me, too!" Henry agreed, falling on the floor to howl his fears.

"Melody," Emily said, tugging on Melody's hand.

"What is it?" Melody asked, kneeling down.

"There wasn't any driver in that truck," the little girl whispered.

"I didn't see one, either," Melody confessed.

"Is the truck a monster?" Emily asked tremulously, "like in a scary movie?"

"The truck isn't a monster, honey," Melody assured her. "Trucks can't be monsters."

"Then how did the truck drive all by itself?" Emily asked.

"I don't know," Melody admitted.

"I want my mommy! I want my mommy!" Henry yelled over and over, his face turning red from the strain.

"I want my mommy, too," Emily said, tears falling down her cheeks. "I don't want to come here anymore. I hate it here."

Melody hugged the little girl. *Who can blame her for hating it here*, she thought to herself. *First someone tries to kidnap her, then a truck comes careening through the daycare center. I wouldn't want to come here, either!*

"The police are on their way," Mrs. Plant told Melody.

"What should we do about the children?" Melody asked.

"Take them outside to the playground," Mrs. Plant said. "It may not be safe in here. If I thought we could reach all their parents to come and pick them up, I would, but I know we can't."

She looked over at the truck and shook her head. "This is a terrible tragedy. If we have to close down, what will happen to the children? And what will happen to my job?"

And to Tarshea's job, Melody thought. *She's supposed to call me at the Inn tonight and she's supposed to come back to work tomorrow. What if she doesn't even have a job to come back to?*

Melody and Mrs. Plant ushered all the kids out to the playground, and they did their best to distract them while they waited for the police. Melody was telling a group of kids a story about a fairy princess while they munched on graham crackers, when two police officers walked into the playground.

And one of them looked just like JD.

"Ma'am," JD said, nodding at Mrs. Plant, then at Melody. "You reported an accident? I'm State Officer Dean, and this is State Officer Hendricks."

Melody smiled at JD. Up in Teen Heaven he had never admitted that he really was James Dean, but clearly he had just admitted it!

"Officer *Dean*?" Melody repeated pointedly.

"Yes, ma'am," JD said. "Dean James is my full name, actually. Dean is my first name. I like to use my first name when I'm on calls with kids. It makes them more comfortable."

"And I'm Officer Hendricks," the tall, slender, African-American officer standing next to JD put in.

Melody blinked, and stared at the other policeman. Hadn't her Aunt Charlotte back in Detroit had a massive crush on a wonderful rock singer and guitarist named Jimi Hendrix? And hadn't Jimi Hendrix died young or something?

"Yes, Officers, thank you for coming so promptly," Mrs. Plant said, not noticing anything unusual. "Well, as you can see, a pickup truck ran into the daycare center!"

"Are all the kids all right?" JD asked.

"Yes, thank God," Mrs. Plant said.

"Mr. Policeman," Emily said, sidling over to Melody.

"Yes?" JD asked.

"There wasn't a driver in the truck. Me and Melody saw. Right, Melody?"

"Right," Melody agreed.

"Driver must have jumped out," Officer Hendricks said, taking out an official police pad and a pen. "We're here to take a complete report."

"I suppose I should call a towing service," Mrs. Plant said nervously.

"No need, ma'am," JD said. "It's already taken care of."

"And we'll have to arrange to have the front of the daycare fixed," Mrs. Plant went on, practically wringing her hands with anxiety. "It isn't safe for the children. But we don't have that kind of money, and the insurance will take so long to pay..."

"Repair service is on their way, ma'am," JD said.

Mrs. Plant gawked at him. "But... how can that be?"

"I took the liberty of arranging it for you," JD said. "After you called 911 and told us what happened."

"But... but..." Mrs. Plant sputtered.

"The Heavenly Hammers should be showing

up any moment," Officer Hendricks explained. "Wonderful company. From, uh, Vermont. And they don't mind waiting until things work out with your insurance to get paid."

"It must be some kind of miracle!" Mrs. Plant exclaimed.

"Yes, ma'am, you might say that," JD agreed.

The phone inside the daycare rang.

"I'll get it," Melody said. "Excuse me." She ran inside and left Mrs. Plant to give the "officers" a report on what had happened, the kids all gathered around listening avidly.

"Hello?" Melody said breathlessly, snatching up the phone.

"You did good, babe," came JD's voice through the phone.

"JD?" Melody asked in shock. "But . . . but . . . you're outside right now, pretending to be a policeman!"

"You must admit, I look fine in a uniform," JD said.

"But how can you be out there and on the phone at the same time?"

"One of my better tricks, don't you think?" JD asked. "I am getting *so* good!"

"And I am getting *so* confused!" Melody admitted, her brow furrowing. "JD, what happened with that truck? Did Deep Sixers do it?"

"Affirmative," JD said. "Payton Fire, also known as Kevin Cravens, also known by a lot of other names that even I will not utter, fixed the accelerator so that the pedal was pushed to the metal, if you catch my drift. Then the hideous creature steered it toward you and jumped out before you could see him."

"But he could have killed Emily!" Melody cried.

"No kidding," JD agreed.

"But why?" Melody exclaimed. "Why would they want to hurt that beautiful little girl?"

"Nothing personal," JD said. "They want to mess up anyone protected by an Angel. That's the way it works."

"What if I hadn't been able to save her?" Melody whispered, her hands trembling on the phone.

"But you did," JD pointed out. "You did good. Hey, listen, as soon as I hang up, the phone rings again. It's Tarshea. She's finished her test."

"I thought she was going to call me at the Inn tonight."

"Well, she's done, so we're moving on to plan B. You ready to come home, Angel?"

"So ready," Melody said fervently. Then she had a terrible thought. "Oh, but will the Deep Sixers still come after Emily after I'm gone?"

"Negative," JD assured her. "The Angel leaves, the Evil Forces turn their attention elsewhere. She's safe now."

"Well, then, I'm definitely ready to come home," Melody said.

"Cool," JD said. "So, go be real nice to those two really fine officers of the law, and I'll see you shortly."

"JD, one thing!" Melody said quickly.

"And that would be?"

"The other officer out there," Melody began. "He wouldn't be . . . Jimi Hendrix, would he?"

"You mean *the* Jimi Hendrix who just happened to be the greatest guitarist of all time, *the*

Jimi Hendrix who mesmerized Woodstock with his unbelievably fine rendition of 'The Star Spangled Banner'? The one who died way before his time, with serious life lessons he still needed to learn?"

"I think so," Melody said.

"Hey, how would I know?" JD asked. "I was already dead by then! Later!"

"But *why* do you have to leave?" Emily asked plaintively.

It was a half hour later, the "officers" had left, Melody had filled a shocked Tarshea in on everything that had happened, and now she was saying good-bye to the little girl she had come to love. Already she felt that strange shimmery sensation that meant her body would soon leave the Earth. Since Tarshea had told her she was coming right over, she knew that Mrs. Plant would have help, and she was free to go.

"Because I don't belong here," Melody explained gently.

"But you could move here," Emily said. "You could live with me and Meredith and Mommy!"

Melody smiled and hugged the little girl close. "I'm sorry, but I can't."

"Will you come visit me?" Emily asked in a small voice.

"I'll always be with you," Melody said. She touched the little girl gently, just over her heart. "In here. In your heart."

I know why you're leaving," Emily said, her face changing. "I just figured it out!"

"No, sweetie, you couldn't understand—"

Could Emily really suspect me? Melody thought quickly.

"It's because you're a TV star, and you have to go back to your show, right?" Emily said.

Melody's jaw hung open in shock. "I . . . I . . ." she stammered, not knowing what to say, thinking of her own performance she'd watched with JD on the EarthScope.

Chills jumped down Melody's spine, and she hugged the little girl again. "It'll be our secret, okay?"

"Okay," Emily said. She was smiling now. "I knew you were too beautiful to be just an ordinary girl."

"Tarshea is on her way over here," Melody said. "She missed you a lot."

"Tarshea is nice," Emily said.

"Will you tell Meredith I said good-bye?" Melody asked.

"She'll miss you, too," Emily said solemnly.

Melody hugged the little girl one last time. The shimmery feeling was growing, and she knew the time had come. "I love you, Emily," she whispered. "Always remember that I love you."

Then she began to walk away from the little girl, waved one last time, and when she passed behind some bushes, she simply disappeared.

"Melody!" Cisco cried, as Melody materialized back in their suite in Teen Heaven. "You're back!"

"We missed you," Nicole said, rushing over to give Melody a hug. "Did you finish your assignment?"

"Yeah," Melody said, sitting down on her bed, since she felt a little dizzy. "Wow, this popping from one world to another is really incredible, isn't it?"

"It defies every law of physics as we know it," Nicole said solemnly.

"Don't mention anything that is an actual school subject, I beg you," Cisco said, plopping down on her own bed. Her large black and white cat, Julius, immediately jumped into her lap. "So, how did it go? Were you a hit?"

"It was incredible," Melody said, shaking her head. "The Deep Sixers were after me, and I had to save this wonderful little girl, and—"

There was a knock on the door.

"Oh, no, it's got to be Celeste," Cisco moaned. "Please, can we just ignore it?"

"I'll tell her we're busy," Nicole said, going to the door.

But it wasn't Celeste. It was Chaz.

"Melody?"

She stood up and stared at her boyfriend, her boyfriend who had betrayed her with Scarlett Whitmore.

"JD told me you were back," Chaz said.

Melody nodded carefully.

"So . . . can we talk?" Chaz asked her. "Privately?"

"You can talk in front of my best friends," Melody said staunchly.

Chaz walked into the room, looking uncertain. "I feel kind of funny . . ."

"Hey, we'll make ourselves scarce," Cisco said, jumping up from her bed. "Nic, let's go over to Rock Around the Cloud and get a burger or something."

"Will you meet us there later?" Nicole asked Melody.

"All right," Melody agreed.

Cisco stopped and hugged Melody again. "We're really glad you're home."

Cisco and Nicole took off, and Melody and Chaz stared at each other uncomfortably.

"So, what did you want to say to me?" Melody asked stiffly.

"About Scarlett . . ." Chaz began.

"You don't have to tell me," Melody said. "I already know. You fell in love with her while I was on assignment. She's completely changed from the brat she was on Earth, and she's really pretty and really nice, and you just couldn't help yourself, right?"

Chaz looked shocked. "Did you do drugs while you were Down Below or something?"

"Of course not," Melody replied. "I'm just telling you what I already know."

"What you know is nothing!" Chaz exclaimed. "I'm not in love with Scarlett!"

"You're not?" Melody asked in a small voice.

"I'm not even sure I really like her yet," Chaz said. "I mean, she's been really nice lately, but how do I know if that's for real?"

"But . . . but every time I saw you, she was with you! And you looked so close . . ."

"She just always seemed to show up right before you did!" Chaz said. "It was really weird!"

"You mean you're not . . . dating her?"

"Of course not!" Chaz said. "Why would I

date her when I'm in love with you?"

Happiness flooded Melody's heart. "You're—?"

"Oh, Mel," Chaz said, "the only problem I have is that you have so little faith in me. In us."

"But I was so sure..." Melody began.

"And you were so wrong," Chaz said firmly. He crossed the room to her and looked deep into her eyes. "Mel, please, tell me that you have enough faith in me so that this won't happen again."

"I'll try," Melody said meekly.

"Because jealousy is like this poison, you know?" Chaz went on earnestly. "I mean, we're both going to assignments Down Below, and we both have our own life, so to speak. We don't spend every single second together, so we gotta learn to have faith in each other!"

"You're right," Melody said. "I'm so sorry—"

Chaz wrapped his arms around her. "Forget the apologies," he said huskily. "Just trust me, Mel. And I'll trust you too, okay?"

"Okay," Melody whispered. She tilted her head up to his, and Chaz gave her the sweetest kiss in the world.

"You know, I love a happy ending," JD said, appearing on top of the CD player, his legs crossed.

"Hey, JD, this is kind of a private moment," Chaz pointed out.

"No prob," JD agreed. "Just want to set a couple of things straight before I'm outta here. So, Mel, learn anything Down Below?"

Melody thought a moment. "That I'm brave enough... maybe... to be a Teen Angel?" she asked tentatively.

"Good one!" JD agreed. "Learn anything about Chaz?"

"He wasn't Down Below," Melody replied, puzzled.

"Yeah, babe, of that I am totally aware," JD agreed. "Which is why you had a hard time. Am I right or am I right?"

It was like a lightbulb going off in Melody's head. "You made sure Scarlett was around Chaz every time I came back up, didn't you?"

"Guilty as charged," JD agreed.

"But why?" Chaz asked.

"Ask Melody," JD suggested.

"Because he wanted me to learn to trust you," Melody realized. "And I failed."

"True," JD said.

"So my mission was a failure then," Melody said slowly.

"Not entirely," JD said, standing up and stretching. He pulled a box of chocolate-covered raisins out of his back pocket, and poured himself a handful. "Down Below you did great work," JD explained. "Up here you kinda washed out."

"I'm sorry," Melody said meekly.

"Can the apologies, Mel," JD said. "The Big Guy doesn't ask for perfection. The Big Guy asks that we work *toward* perfection, okay?"

"Okay," Melody agreed.

"And when you love someone, and they love you, you gotta learn to trust," JD added.

"I'll try my best," Melody promised.

"Cool! Then I'm outta here. Have a heavenly evening, you two, and—"

"Just one last thing, JD," Melody interrupted.

"Ask away," JD said.

"When Kevin tried to snatch Emily, when I felt like I was frozen to the spot and I couldn't move or speak, did Deep Six do that?" Melody asked.

"Nope," JD replied.

"Then . . . who?" Melody asked. "What?"

JD cocked his head at her. "Fear is a powerful force, Mel."

She thought a moment. "You mean . . . I did it to myself? Because I was so afraid?"

"That's about the size of it," JD agreed.

"But that's terrible!" Melody cried. "How can I call myself any kind of an angel! It took the voice of the Big Guy to unfreeze me!"

"Wrong," JD said blithely.

"But it can't be wrong!" Melody insisted. "I was stuck, petrified with fear, and then I heard this voice telling me I could do it, that I had the power . . ."

JD nodded at her slowly, a small smile on his lips. "Whose voice was it, Mel?"

And suddenly, she knew. With a thousand percent of her knowing, she finally understood.

The voice had been her own.

"It was my voice, wasn't it," Melody said, her hands over her heart.

"Some voice, huh?" JD said with approval. "That was your highest voice, your best self, the self you are becoming . . . seeing with your heart, is what the Big Guy calls it. Kinda awesome, when you think about it." JD strolled over to Melody, and planted a kiss on her forehead. "Good work, Angel." Then he snapped his fingers, and disappeared.

"What was that all about?" Chaz asked in confusion.

"I'll tell you everything," Melody said, her eyes shining with happiness. "Oh, Chaz, it's so wonderful!"

"What is?" he asked. "That we're together again?"

"That," Melody agreed. "But I just learned something. There's a little bit of the Big Guy inside of me—inside of all of us, I guess."

"Yeah, I believe that," Chaz agreed, putting his arms around her again.

"It's true," Melody said, tears of happiness forming in her eyes. "Now I know it's true. I have the faith. And I have the power. The power is . . . believing in me. Isn't that fantastic?"

Instead of waiting for an answer, she threw her arms around Chaz and pulled him to her something she had never, ever had the nerve to do before.

And then she kissed him, a dazzling, wonderful, incredible kiss, full of life and love.

And all around her, the heavens danced.

Hey Angel Sisters—

Woah, baby. The letters are flying in about the "Teen Angel" books. And they are great! Remember, if you'd like your letter to Jeff and me to be considered for publication, tell me, and if you'd like your letter to be kept private, tell me that, too.

If your letter ends up getting published, like some of these that follow, Jeff and I will send you an autographed copy of that "Teen Angels" book, for free!

So let's go to the mailbag and see a little of what's come in lately: Cheryl H. of Richmond, Kentucky, made her own awesome "Teen Angels" stationary and said the first book made her cry. Vanessa C. of Sweetser, Indiana, loved *Teen Angels: Love Never Dies* and said the book touched her heart and that she believes angels are all around us. Juliet B. of Los Angeles, California, said she likes the "Teen Angels" books best of anything I've written and loves the guy perspective that Jeff brings. Juliet, we gotta agree with you!

Are there angels among us? We don't know for sure, but one thing writing these books has taught Jeff and me is that even though we're human, we can be angels ourselves, even if we don't always act angelic.

Big trips coming up for Jeff and me: My plays "John Lennon & Me" and "Anne Frank & Me" are being performed in the next few months in seven different theaters around the country. I hope to run into some of you along the way!

Teen Angels are among us. Keep those cards

and letters and photos coming. Find us on the Internet at authorchik@aol.com, and we'll set you up with some online penpals if you'd like. Every letter gets answered, and you get a newsletter, too. You guys are the greatest!

Cherie (with Jeff reading this over my shoulder)

> Cherie & Jeff
> P.O. Box 150326
> Nashville, TN 07215

"Your books are some of the best books I've read in a while! I love them and can't pull my eyes from the page as they get closer to the end. They're full of surprises—good surprises at that."

> A. Dujmovich
> Katy, Texas

"Great stuff! By the end, I was really teary-eyed ... a cool sentimental ending, with a great emotional payoff at the end. Your books are different from all the others. Thank you, thank you, THANK YOU!"

> M. McManus
> Trenton, New Jersey

"I just love your books. They are great! You are the best author ever. I feel like I know every character. I read all the time ... maybe one day I'll be an author too! Keep the great books coming."

> S. Paterson
> Pensacola, Florida

"I just wanted to write and say I think you're a wonderful author and thank you for getting me into reading. Because before I found your books I hated to read, but now I love it."
                    C. Martin
                    Mt. Pleasant, South Carolina